RAKE

A NOVEL

SCOTT PHILLIPS

COUNTERPOINT
BERKELEY

Rake

Library of Congress Cataloging-in-Publication data is available
ISBN 978-1-61902-151-8

Cover design by Michael Fusco, M+E/Michael Fusco Design
Interior design by Gerilyn Attebery

COUNTERPOINT
1919 Fifth Street
Berkeley, CA 94710
www.counterpointpress.com

Printed in the United States of America
Distributed by Publishers Group West

10 9 8 7 6 5 4 3 2 1

"That's a lot of superstitious baloney."
"Superstitious, maybe. Baloney, maybe not."

—David Manners and Bela Lugosi,
in *The Black Cat*, based on a story by Edgar Allan Poe,
written by Edgar G. Ulmer and Peter Ruric,
and directed by Ulmer

RAKE

VENDREDI, TREIZE MAI

IT'S MAYBE 2:00 OR 3:00 AM WHEN I AWAKEN to the smell of Esmée still clinging to the sheets and to the unmistakable sensation of someone's presence in the apartment. Esmée left hours ago, and though the lights are out and I hear nothing but the sound of the air conditioner cycling, my instincts tell me I'm right. Sliding off of the bed as quietly as I can, I crouch and try to remember where I put my telescoping baton. All right, got it, my inside sportjacket pocket, but where's the jacket?

Too late for that anyway. Someone's standing in the doorway of the bedroom, and I don't know if he sees me or not.

I'm next to an end table, and as quietly as possible I run my hand over it, trying to remember whether there's anything on it that might be used as a weapon. My hand clasps something oblong, made of stone and weighing a good two and a half kilos.

I'm creeping toward the figure when a flash goes off, the sound of gunfire mostly muffled by a silencer. A moment later my would-be killer flicks on the light switch and reveals himself: Claude Guiteau has come to do his own dirty work, using his own two hands. I'm almost proud of the old boy as I swing my blunt object down over his head. This all takes place in the split second he stands there puzzling over the fact that there's no corpse in the bed, just a bullet hole in the pillow.

Once down, he's not completely out. The pistol's on the floor, though, and for a few slow moments he gazes in blurry puzzlement up at me. Then to my relief, he passes out; I don't want to hit him again, having realized that I've bludgeoned him with a very fine piece of antique jade, another blow to which might snap it.

I set about restraining him and consider my options. What, for example, will happen if I call the cops? Scandal would lead to some really first-rate publicity, which would in no way harm my bankability; but with Claude in prison our project would stall, maybe fatally.

Kill him? Not here, in his own apartment, certainly. It occurs to me that, given his line of work, he might have the kind of enemies who'd pay to see him dead, might even pay to have him handed over alive in order to kill him themselves in some exquisitely horrible and painful manner.

But having the man tortured to death seems unsporting. After all, this attempt on my life would have been instantaneous and quite possibly painless, had he succeeded. I dial Fred, whose business this is whether he knows it or not, and tell him to come over immediately and to be discreet about it. Take a cab and get out a couple of blocks away, I tell him.

"You want to have a story meeting now? At three-fifteen in the morning?"

"Not a story meeting. This is more of a finance meeting. Now get your ass on over here."

• • •

By the time he arrives I have poor Claude trussed up like a prize steer at a rodeo. In one unlocked drawer in the closet was a plentiful supply of ropes, gags, nipple clips, and so on, something I'll have to question Esmée about at some future date. For the moment, however, they're perfect for restraining Claude, who has yet to regain consciousness. When Fred walks into the kitchen he finds Claude unconscious and tightly bound to the chair with a bright sky-blue ball gag stuffed in his mouth.

"Holy shit," Fred says.

"Yeah. You got any ideas for getting rid of the son of a bitch?"

"Who is he?"

I'd forgotten Fred hadn't met him yet. "Esmée's husband."

His voice rises about an octave. "Our backer?"

"He tried to kill me."

"What for?"

"I guess he found out I was banging his old lady."

"Goddamn it." He raises his hands to his temples and spins around once in disbelief at my carelessness. "Didn't I warn you not to do that? Shit. You think he's going to put up the money now?"

I had given that a fair amount of thought while preparing for Fred's arrival. He wasn't going to put up any money now, that was for sure. "That's what you're here for. You're the brains of the outfit."

He stares at Claude for a minute, the cogs rolling in his head, and I feel a sudden burst of confidence in him. Whatever I've done, Fred's the guy who's going to make it better.

"Happy Friday the thirteenth," I tell him. "I do have one small suggestion. I know a girl who has access to a meat locker."

He thinks it over, seems to approve. He's a smart fellow, cautious and analytical, and if he approves of the idea, I feel certain it's a sound one.

Maybe, I think, I'm home free. Maybe the curse of the calendar did its damage to Claude rather than to me. I am, after all, a member of a superstitious profession, an avoider of black cats and hats left on the bed and broken mirrors. Perhaps the gods of superstitions have rewarded me for all my years of fidelity.

• • •

Or maybe I'm fucked.

FIFTEEN DAYS EARLIER: JEUDI, VINGT-HUIT AVRIL

YOU KNOW ME, OR MORE PRECISELY YOU have the distinct impression that you know me; it probably amounts to the same thing, from your point of view at least. For five years I played Dr. Crandall Taylor, dissolute, randy, ne'er-do-well bastard son of Senator Harwood Taylor on an American soap opera called *Ventura County*. No one paid the show any attention at all back home, where it ran five days a week at eleven in the morning, watched only by the loneliest and horniest of housewives and the laziest of college students. In Europe, though, they had the bright idea of running us in the evening, right at the start of prime time, and to everyone's surprise we turned into a massive hit. With each one-hour episode cut in half, our five-year run will last ten over here, and though the show's been out of production for three years, we're still a success in most of Europe, with several years' worth of episodes still to run.

And I was the star of the thing. I can't cross the street in Paris without somebody doing a double-take and calling out "Hey,

Crandall," or have dinner in a nice restaurant without having to interrupt my conversation and chat with some well-meaning, star-struck viewer.

This is the point in the story where you'll be expecting the usual celebrity whine about loss of privacy, intrusive fans, and how much I wish I had my anonymity back. You're thinking how happy you'd be, how if you were wallowing in money and pussy and adulation from complete strangers, if you could just walk right into some club with a line stretching down the sidewalk, if the chef always wanted to send you something a little extra just for doing him the favor of showing up at his restaurant, if people were scrambling to get you to make a CD or a new TV show and pay you even more money and make you even more famous, well, that'd be just fine with you.

So I'm going to surprise you right here and leave out the bitching. Sure, sometimes it's a drag when someone interrupts a meal, but so fucking what? I'm an actor. What exactly did I think I was signing up for here? It's great, getting treated like something special. Free stuff, brazen women—especially women who are normally demure but who get sexually aggressive when they see a celebrity—preferred seating everywhere I go: yeah, this is pretty much the life you imagine it is. And it's great.

• • •

For example: Not long ago I was spending a pleasant evening in a nightclub off the Étoile. The bouncer let me in without paying, management sent over a complimentary bottle of Veuve Clicquot, and as I scanned the crowd for some woman who might want to come back to my suite, an attractive lady came over to my table, leaned down to whisper in my ear, and then casually suggested I might want to fuck her while her husband watched. She was in her early thirties, wearing a blue minidress and high-heeled shoes that in the dim light of the club seemed to match it. Her face promised something wild, with a sharp little nose and a crooked smile and big, round doe eyes that didn't ever seem to blink. Her hair was cut razor-close at the sides, and as she spoke to me she was making little rotating motions with her pelvis as though she were already gearing up for it, and I thought what the hell?

So the three of us headed for their apartment in the sixteenth, with hubby driving while I fingerbanged milady in the backseat. I was a little disappointed that she wasn't wearing underwear, since one of my favorite moments when fucking a girl for the first time is that moment when your fingers cross that elastic Maginot Line of her panties. She was making a hell of a lot of noise while I did it, and our driver drove without betraying any reaction whatsoever. I suppose that was part of the thrill of it for the poor bastard.

Their apartment was furnished like the palace at Versailles, all really old stuff, and quality, too. The paintings on the wall dated from about the seventeenth century to the late nineteenth and ranged from portraiture to landscapes executed in an academic style. (Did I mention I had a master's degree in theater arts from Southwest Minnesota State University? And here you were thinking that actors were dolts.) The nanny came out to greet us, a British girl of twenty with zits and thick glasses who I could tell was going to be a knockout in about five years once the adolescence drained out of her. She recognized me immediately and blushed, and without commenting on my presence gave my hosts a report on the evening's activities. Their children had behaved admirably, and apparently the youngest had taken several steps unassisted.

Once the girl was dismissed I followed the couple back to their bedroom. The wife instructed the husband in rather stern terms to sit in what looked to me like a genuine Louis XV fauteuil and not say a word. Then she went down on me for a minute or two, and when I was erect she leapt onto the bed, on all fours, and said, "Give me what my husband can't."

As I fucked her in various and sundry positions she verbally abused her husband in the third person, excoriating his manhood, his potency, his decency as a human being, and I found myself wondering how these two had managed to find each other, and whether the whole routine had started out as his thing or hers. In any case, I didn't mind being watched, and when at length I finished I looked over at him. He'd shot a load onto the ceiling, which seemed to disprove his wife's claims of impotence.

"My God, you must think I'm the world's worst hostess, I haven't even offered you anything to drink," she said, slipping her dress back on as her husband mopped up his mess with a tissue. We moved into the salon and she rang for a maid in the sort of uniform I didn't think housemaids really wore any more.

"Fetch monsieur a whisky," my hostess said, and the maid, whose uniform, I noted, was a bit too short to be really practical, scooted out of the room. I supposed that part of her duties involved some other pedestrian sexual fantasy: spanking the maid, or some sort of infantilism. Perhaps she did double duty as a naughty nurse. "I'm Marie-France," the wife said, "and this is my husband, Gérard."

"Pleased to meet you," I said, without bothering to pretend they didn't already know me.

"What brings you to Paris?" the happily cuckolded Gérard said.

"Trying to get a film set up."

"How exciting," Marie-France said.

This was true, more or less. I had a couple of contacts who'd expressed interest in trying to raise money for a feature. So far, though, they were full of hot air and not one of them had the wherewithal to get a movie made. One of them even suggested that I commission a screenplay myself, after which he'd help me get it made. No thanks, asshole.

"I hope we'll see you again. Perhaps we can visit the set when you're filming," she said after the maid had brought me my whisky.

"That would be fine with me." I produced a *carte de visite* and handed it to her. She made a point of having her fingertips linger on mine, as though we'd just met and were flirting. It was kind of charming, but the number on the *carte* was from a different hotel and a previous visit, and I didn't imagine I'd be seeing them again.

VENDREDI, VINGT-NEUF AVRIL

NEXT MORNING I GOT UP EARLY AND HAD coffee and a croissant on the terrace of a café down the avenue from the hotel. It was a Friday, the sidewalk was crowded, and I enjoyed the expressions of surprise on the passersby as they registered my presence. One sweet-looking woman of eighty or so stopped, excused herself, and asked whether I was or was not, in fact, Dr. Crandall Taylor.

"I play him on television," I replied.

"I thought that was you. I have a bone to pick with you, young man."

"What's that?"

She drew herself up straight, took a deep breath, and cocked her head at an angle that suggested a stinging lecture was about to be delivered. I suspected she'd been a schoolteacher once.

"You've made a terrible, foolish mistake," she said. "That young woman was the love of your life, and you let her go over a foolish dalliance with that other doctor. A dalliance that you provoked, may I add, by your own repeated infidelities."

I toyed with the idea of trying to explain the difference between myself and the character I played, but the old dear was clearly out of her mind. I merely nodded, trying to remember what happened after Constance had her affair with Dr. Corby. Had Taylor taken her back immediately, or had there been a marriage or three in between? It was a bit of a blur at this remove.

"You're absolutely right, madame," I said. "Constance means everything to me. I will try to act on your advice."

She squinted. "You sound funny. Like an American."

"Everybody sounds different on television."

She nodded her acceptance of the theory, then rolled up the left sleeve of her sweater. "What do you make of that?" she asked, pointing to a purplish splotch that looked remarkably like the other purplish splotches in its vicinity, as well as those on her face, neck, and hands.

I squinted and frowned, brought my forefinger to my lips to invoke the diagnostic process. I might not have had it in me to be a real doctor, but I would have had a kick-ass bedside manner. Real doctors have told me this, and a young allergist I once consulted told me he'd been such a fan of the show in med school that he'd modeled some of his gestures and tics after my own. That was one of my proudest moments as an actor.

"How long have you had this?" I asked, my tone midway between concern and reassurance.

"I don't know," she said. "A while."

"I'd like you to see your regular doctor as soon as possible. He knows your history better than I do. And once he's examined it, you come back here and let me know what he says."

"Here? To the café?"

"I'm here most mornings."

She nodded in a grave manner and proceeded on her way.

This wasn't the first time I'd received such advice from a stranger. Constance, the love of the good doctor's turbulent life, was incarnated on the TV screen by the lovely Tasha Coltrane, and I always thought one reason the viewers had so much emotion invested in that romance was that Tasha and I were fast friends off the set. A great number of those viewers assumed that we were actually lovers offscreen, which might have happened if not for the impediment of Tasha's lesbianism; I guess part of our rapport must have been based on our ability to sit around for hours and talk about pussy.

One actress I did fuck off and on over the show's years in production was Becky Tremaine, who played Dr. Taylor's half-sister Vanessa. I have discovered that fans of the show don't take well to this knowledge; they react to the news as though we were actual siblings, and so I made it a point never to travel with her. (I don't even want to think about what would happen if they found out I'd also fucked Frances Lannigan, who played Dr. Taylor's mother. In fact, I was pretty careful to keep Becky in the dark about that one.) Becky's own mother was Lucy Tremaine, a television star of the sixties whose name is better known in the States than here, and her stepfather directed half the sitcoms ever aired.

Off the top of my head, here are the other cast members I slept with: Alicia Bertoldi, who played Senator Taylor's third wife; Sally Collins, who intermittently played a biker chick for two or three seasons and, though she was in reality a nice Catholic girl, ended up killing herself for reasons never clear to me; Serena Hopp, who played the dual roles of Senator Taylor's fourth wife and her twin sister; Annette Dillingsworth, who played the hospital's chief administrator and who, at fifteen years my senior, could drink and coke me under the table and who once gave me a black eye during a bout of unusually rambunctious sexual experimentation.

And then there was Ginny De Kalb, a former Miss Missouri who did a couple of years on the show as Trina Vail, the polymorphously perverse owner of a horse farm. Ginny was crushed when her role was recast, but she should have seen it coming—her character's story line involved a sex change, and though there are any number of actresses who could have played Trina in her post-op incarnation as Buck Vail, Ginny was not one of them. She surprised all of us when she turned to online erotica and made a fortune starring in and promoting a series of downloadable adult entertainments. She even did one video that played on the Trina/Buck sex change in which she, in a manner of speaking, went and fucked herself. Though it's doubtful that there was much of an intersection between her soap opera fans and the admirers of her pornographic oeuvre, I for one was amused and aroused by the video, so much so that I looked her up and carried on a reasonably torrid affair with her for a year or so.

• • •

Anyway, those are the ones that come to me off the top of my head. Looking back, it was a hell of a fun show to work on. Two seasons in I nearly lost the role when sweet, Catholic Sally Collins's husband walked in on us in her dressing room. I was fucking her from behind and she was shouting about what a dirty, dirty girl she was, and he grabbed the tennis racket she kept by the door and came swinging at me. I broke his arm and his collarbone before Sally's screaming stopped me.

It could have been argued that he was provoked into violence by the sight of his wife (who was pregnant at the time, though not, as far as I could tell, by me) being fucked by another man, and that indeed was the line the producers of the show took with my poor, long-suffering agent, threatening to fire me.

I was already a fan favorite, though, and we settled with Sally's husband out of court; I put up a hundred grand and the production company came up with two hundred and fifty. At the insistence of the Legal Department I took six months of anger management classes, which provided me with some interesting insights into my sometimes violent personal history. When I boasted that it had been more than fifteen years since my last arrest for assault and battery, the rest of my group laughed along with the instructor-counselor, and for a moment I was baffled and hurt, until I understood that they thought I was joking. Hell, I wasn't angry, hadn't been for years. All I'd done was defend myself against an attacker—too zealously, perhaps, but justifiably.

As for the irate husband, he disappeared into the woodwork, leaving Sally to raise their child alone. As a good Catholic girl, she took the divorce hard; after that she tended to avoid me away from the set, but I believe the drama of our off-camera story had an incendiary effect on our subsequent scenes together, lending a distraught quality to her performance that her modest, inborn level of talent couldn't have provided. Now that I think of her I can't help wondering what happened to that kid of hers.

SAMEDI, TRENTE AVRIL

THE NEXT NIGHT THE NETWORK LIAISON—Jean-Pierre by name—took me to a play at a small theater starring Nicolas Aurel, my vocal doppelganger on *Ventura County.*

Accompanying us was a certain Marie-Laure Vasquès, one of Jean-Pierre's bosses at the network. Well into her forties, with long legs and black hair cut in a Louise Brooks bob, she affected delight at meeting me and chain-smoked in the car on the way to the theater. She had one of those faces that are hard to classify at first—she was either an idiosyncratic beauty or a little funny looking, with a nose that was at once rather long for her face and unusually slim, and eyes set wider apart than she probably would have preferred. Given her position at the network I made sure to casually mention my mission in France of getting a movie made, insinuating that it was practically a done deal and resisting the temptation to suggest overtly that there was still time for the network to invest in it.

She was very interested in the activities of my fellow cast members since the show had wrapped. Why she gave a shit I don't know; I was the only one who spoke French, the one who came over and did publicity every year and without their having to hire an interpreter. But I filled her in on the retirements (three), the moves to other soaps (most of them), the sitcom role (Alicia), the three movie roles (including a big one for Becky), and the untimely death (poor Sally).

She told me she'd worked in L.A. a few years back for our overseas syndicator and claimed some responsibility for the show's having been picked up in prime time here.

"I have you to thank, then," I said and regretted not having paid more attention when Jean-Pierre had introduced us outside the hotel. What was her official title?

She smiled, a radiant, genuine expression that made her suddenly even more attractive than before, and noting the ring on her left hand, I wondered how hard it would be to get her into bed, and whether or not that would be a good idea, business-wise. "You're really a very good actor," she said, cementing my desire. "I saw you in that Garry Marshall movie last year."

"Oh," I said, and Jean-Pierre, who knows me well enough to poke a little fun, smirked at the mention of it.

"Don't misunderstand me, the picture was a piece of shit," she said, "but you were quite good."

"You're too kind."

"Not at all. Have you got anything lined up here? Besides your own film, I mean?"

Feeling foolish, I tried to downplay my entirely conjectural film project. "It's really in the embryonic stages at the moment. And, no, I don't have anything else lined up."

"Is there a script?"

"I'm collaborating on one with a young French screenwriter."

She crossed her legs and nodded. "Bring him in for a meeting, maybe we can make something happen. In the meantime there's a role on one of our cop shows that would be perfect for you. It was written for an Englishman but it could easily be an American."

"I can play British, of course," I said, bristling, as we stopped in front of the theater.

• • •

I'd met Nicolas a few times and had always been impressed by his talents as a voice artist, but this was the first time I'd seen him act. He was a handsome young fellow with terrific stage presence, hulking and with a real sense of physical menace, even though he wasn't really very large. My real-life tendencies as a brawler besides, I've been in my share of fights onstage and pride myself on being able to spot a poorly faked one; there was a moment in a third-act fight scene, though, when I thought he'd really broken his cast mate's jaw.

The play was mediocre but the actors were good, and afterward we went out for a bite with Nicolas, his wife, and a couple of the actresses, both of whom paid me a great deal of attention over several platters of oysters. As one of the actresses howled in exaggerated laughter at an anecdote I'd just told, Nicolas nudged me and whispered that if I were to take the young lady in question home with me I wouldn't be disappointed. I reserved my most solicitous attentions for Marie-Laure, however, and began considering at what point it would be politically wise to invite her up to my suite, tonight or some other evening after dinner.

As it happened, when Jean-Pierre dropped me off at the hotel she told him she wanted a cocktail with me and would catch a cab home. The almost predatory look on her face as we walked arm in arm to the hotel bar sent a little chill down my spine and excited me even more than before.

DIMANCHE, PREMIER MAI

I WAS STUCK. I NEEDED A STORY FOR A MOVIE, and I needed to find a French screenwriter for Marie-Laure's meeting. And I needed one who wouldn't be asking for money up front, which precluded my doing it through an agent. It occurred to me that I might be able to adapt a book myself, lifting the dialogue verbatim and transferring the descriptive action from the past to the present tense (this is how John Huston adapted *The Maltese Falcon*, or rather how his secretary did it; before leaving town for the weekend, he gave her the novel and told her to type it up in screenplay format, and upon his return he found the result perfectly filmable).

But I needed to find a book, a title obscure enough that its author would accept a minimal option or none at all on the promise of a later payday. And I did have every reason to believe that there would be a payoff at some later date.

I wandered off from the hotel with the idea of a walk. I circled the courtyard of the Louvre and the Tuileries and headed across the rue de Rivoli to the arcade and walked along, acknowledging in my amiable but unapproachable manner the cries of recognition from my fellow flaneurs. I passed two English-language booksellers I knew well, but I'd need the book to be in French to start with, as an adaptation and translation together would take me twice the time.

And then I stumbled upon a small bookstore, one that had obviously been around for decades but which had somehow escaped my notice in the past. Noting with satisfaction that the only person inside was the clerk, which would give me the chance to peruse the shelves unmolested by fans, I stepped inside. With a nod to the clerk I began browsing through the fiction section and then the crime section, with the idea that genre books were likely simpler and therefore easier to adapt. My problem was that I didn't know which ones had already been made into films, which ones had been optioned, which ones were unsuitable for adaptation. Judging by the covers alone, they all looked the same.

"Are you interested in books in English?" the bookseller asked me in my native language.

Mildly insulted, I responded in French. "Actually I'm looking for a film property. Do you know offhand whether any of these have been filmed?"

He shook his head. He was a little jug-eared guy with a tendency to move and speak very quickly, and he speed-walked to the back of the store. "No idea. They usually change the titles for the cinema, and they don't always put out a movie edition." He pulled a book from a table. "Here, I'm going to make you a gift of this one."

He opened the book up and, whipping a fountain pen out of his shirt pocket, signed the title page and handed it to me.

"Thanks very much," I said, puzzled and a bit nonplussed at his willingness to hand over store property to a stranger.

"I'm the author," he said, and upon examination of the back flap I found a photographic portrait of the small, bespectacled man before me. Frédéric LaForge, according to the title page.

"What sort of book is it?" I asked, thinking I might have found my source material.

"It's the story of a sexual tourist who travels to Thailand, deliberately gets infected with AIDS, and comes back to France and with equal deliberation infects everyone he can talk into bed, including—especially—his own twin sister."

"His twin sister."

"Right. It's the guilt from their incestuous affair that leads him to seek out prostitutes."

"I imagine it would." I turned to a page in the middle of the book and read a paragraph at random:

> *She came to her usual quick, effortless orgasm, that chipmunk-like yelp I had loved hearing since adolescence, and I gave some thought to delivering her death sentence just at that moment. But something in her eyes as she looked into mine—call it love, call it nostalgia, call it an unconscious plea for a reprieve—made me withdraw and shoot my viscous poison harmlessly onto her belly instead.*

Sadly, this seemed exactly like the kind of art-house movie I had no interest in making. But that didn't mean that my new friend didn't have it in him to write a decent popcorn movie. "Is this your first novel?" I asked.

"It is. I have another I'm two-thirds of the way through, about a brother and sister who murder their parents and have to struggle to be reunited after the juvenile justice system separates them."

Someday I'll have to meet this guy's sister, I thought, she must be a real firecracker. "Have you ever written for the cinema?" I asked.

"No. I'm a prose artist, strictly."

"That's too bad, because thumbing through here I can see that you have a way with dialogue, and I'm looking for a collaborator on a film project."

He shrugged and frowned, eyes on the hardwood floor of the bookshop. "I suppose screenwriting is a craft like any other sort of writing . . ."

I handed him the hotel's card and wrote on the back the name I was staying under. "Give me a call in a day or two and we'll knock some ideas around," I said.

• • •

That night I dined alone in a restaurant near the Palais Royal, an old favorite of mine on a narrow side street connecting the rue de Richelieu and the rue Montpensier. The food was excellent, the service attentive without being obsequious—which is sometimes a problem for the famous—and over a sumptuous cassoulet I was taken back to my college days and the two summers I spent here, during which this restaurant was a weekly indulgence, an escape from dormitory food. The place was under different management now, and I wondered what had become of the couple who once ran it—the wife was one of those women one sees only in France, plain to the point of being nearly homely, and yet possessed of an erotic energy that attracted me back Wednesday after Wednesday as much as the food itself.

I got into a fight in that neighborhood once, during one of those university summers. One of my countrymen had had a few too many beers and was making a spectacle of himself and, in my youthful opinion, was casting a bad light on Americans in general. Having downed a few myself, I told him to shut the fuck up. He and his friends approached me, sneering, and I brought him to his knees with a quick left-right combination, upon which I shoved his two comrades together head-first, then brought them to the ground with a pair of uppercuts.

Was I proud as I strode off that night? I wasn't. I felt I'd just proven that I'd learned nothing from my unfortunate experience in the military, that my supposed commitment to pacifism was just a veneer that might be lifted at any moment when I saw an opportunity for violence.

Now, years later, dining tranquilly in that same neighborhood, I felt a calm and a sense of well-being. It had taken time, but I had learned those lessons. The days of my striking first were behind me.

• • •

Seated at a table across the dining room was a pair of women who looked like they might be sisters, whispering to one another and occasionally sneaking a glance in my direction and giggling. They were attractive, in their late twenties and stylishly dressed, and they finished eating at the same time as I did, so I invited them back to my hotel for a nightcap. They accepted.

LUNDI, DEUX MAI

SISTERS THEY INDEED TURNED OUT TO BE, and they didn't leave my suite until after eleven in the morning, after a rather sumptuous room service breakfast, American style with scrambled eggs and bacon. I had always fantasized about doing a pair of sisters (preferably twins; you can't have everything), and like so many fantasies, the real thing was a bit of a letdown. I won't deny that it was fun, but no more so than going to bed with any other pair of women.

When they were gone I checked my e-mails and found only one I cared to open, from some misguided soul who wanted to write a biographical piece on me for an encyclopedia of American television actors. Though I suspected it to be a prank, I sat down and wrote a wholly fictional autobiographical sketch that suited the image I wished to project:

> *Born July 19—, Newport, R.I. Graduated magna cum laude from Exeter. Graduated from Harvard University with a*

Bachelor of Arts in literary criticism, followed by a PhD from MIT in particle physics. Widowed at the age of twenty-seven in a car wreck on honeymoon, never recovered emotionally, turned to acting as a form of therapy.

I sent it off and wondered what my fans' reaction would be if they knew the truth. Would they be able to reconcile the suave, seductive, intellectual man of medicine with the low-born hell-raiser of my youth? Hell, they'd probably eat it up; people love a hint of scandal, particularly when it involves obstacles overcome. But they weren't going to find out about it.

• • •

Late in the afternoon I took a stroll through the Tuileries to clear my head and perhaps come up with a workable idea. Approaching the Grand Bassin I crossed paths with a pretty, dark-haired girl in her early twenties, dressed in clothes too bulky to say what her body looked like but whose saucy expression made me stop. She pulled a small camera from her purse and dangled it from its strap.

"Do you mind?" she asked in English. "No one's going to believe I saw you."

"I don't mind at all," I answered in French, and I gave her the sexiest, most insouciant smirk I could manage (and the sexy, insouciant smirk is my trademark). When she was done taking the pictures I pointed out that it was the cocktail hour, and I wondered where she was off to in such a hurry.

"Going to meet my boyfriend for a movie."

"Could I interest you in postponing that movie and joining me for a drink?"

She pretended to consider it, then pulled out her cell phone to call the boyfriend and lie about an exam she had to study for.

Three minutes later we grabbed a taxi on the rue de Rivoli and headed for my hotel's bar.

• • •

Her name was Annick, she was a graduate student in American literature, and she was working on a visa application for a year's study in the USA. I offered any help I could provide and spoke of my own youthful experiences in Paris, without mentioning how many years ago that had been (suffice it to say that the lovely Annick hadn't been born yet).

We went over all this in the bar over glasses of wine, and it took only two apiece to convince her that my suite would be a better place to consume a third.

There's a contagious aspect to the thrill some women get from having sex with someone famous, and Annick was as wide-eyed as a marmoset at the prospect. What she lacked in experience she made up for with the flawless body of a twenty-three-year-old, and though her orgasms were faked they were well faked.

"You're very pretty," I told her afterward.

"Pretty? Try beautiful, you'll get further," she said, and laughed.

"It's true, you do cross that line from pretty to beautiful." I looked her over, trying to decide exactly where that line was. I decided it was a certain ruthlessness in her eyes, a sense that with the right amount of prodding she'd be up for just about anything.

"Do you think I'm pretty enough to be on television?"

"More than pretty enough. But it takes more than looks. Those summers I spent here as a student, I was attending plays, doing workshops, memorizing speeches in a language I didn't know that well yet. And then there were years of repertory theater and bit roles before I got famous. But you're still young, certainly young enough to start."

When she challenged me on the point I asked her how quickly I could get a job at the Sorbonne teaching literature.

"That's completely different," she said. "You can't just walk into a university and demand to teach."

I could have continued arguing, but I thought I'd like to see her again sometime, so I conceded the point, and in a little while she went off on her way.

I got dressed and walked out of the hotel, headed in the general direction of the Louvre and thinking I might try to re-create the museum experience of my student days, and then I remembered it was a Monday, the museum closed. Tomorrow would have to do.

MARDI, TROIS MAI

BESIDES THE OBVIOUS CHANGES, STARTING with that glass pyramid, one element of a Louvre visit that had changed was the experience of checking my overcoat: Upon recognizing me, a giddy coat-check lady called a friend in another department, and before long a swarm of museum employees, nearly all female, were lined up for autographs next to the counter, joined by a handful of visitors distracted from the disposition of their outer garments by my surprise presence. I spent the better part of forty-five minutes chatting with them and posing for pictures before the crowd finally dissipated; one plump, ruddy-faced lady, an employee of one of the gift shops, had burst into tears at the sight of me and was only now pulling herself together.

You may wonder why I bother indulging a group of complete strangers. Not all celebrities do, and it would be perfectly easy to blow the first of them off with a curt, phony smile and avoid the rest of them entirely; after all, they'll very likely never run into me again. But that's precisely the point: It's a one-time encounter, and they'll remember it forever. And if I'm a sweetheart, they'll tell everybody that Dr. Crandall Taylor from *Ventura County* is a sweetheart. Conversely, if I'm an asshole . . .

• • •

Once the duties of my station had been discharged, I started, as I always had, with David and Elizabeth Vigée-LeBrun. This was where I had started on my very first visit to the museum, lo, those many years ago, in the company of a woman I was deeply infatuated with and whose background in art history centered on eighteenth- and nineteenth-century French painting. Moving on to Courbet and then to Géricault, I spent a good ten minutes contemplating *The Raft of the Medusa* and nearly unaware of those museumgoers who were contemplating me at the same time. Then on to Ingres, to linger on his wonderfully anatomically incorrect *Odalisque*, she of the half-dozen extra vertebrae and tantalizing smile, a thousand times more beguiling than that of the *Mona Lisa* around the corner.

• • •

After an hour and a half I stopped for a coffee—offered to me without charge by a giggling *serveuse* for whom I'd already signed an autograph at the coat check—and was seized by the urge to see pregnant Gabrielle d'Estrées getting her nipple pinched by that cheeky sister of hers. On the way I stopped to admire the *Winged Nike of Samothrace* and, on a whim, made a quick detour to see the Venus de Milo.

At this point you may be wondering why I'm burdening you with this self-consciously nostalgic tour of the Louvre's Greatest Hits. The point is this: Standing before the Venus de Milo and contemplating her charms as a piece of classical sculpture, as an icon for the ages, I had a banal thought that has come to generations of art-benumbed museumgoers: I wondered what had happened to her arms.

At this point I would have moved on to Henri IV's brazen mistress, but something kept me rooted to the spot. Something was suggesting itself to me, some opportunity trying to claw its way out of my unconscious.

And then some idiot called out, "Crandall!" and I once again found myself surrounded by a crowd suddenly freed by the shouter from their shyness. As I signed autograph after autograph I despaired for my lost spark of inspiration, until finally some bold soul asked me if I was at the Louvre preparing to shoot an episode of the show.

"Not the show," I said, the idea blossoming in the pit of my stomach as I spoke. "A movie."

I had found my subject. I had to get hold of Frédéric right away: We were going to make a movie about the guy who finds the arms of the Venus de Milo. The only question now: comedy or drama?

• • •

On my way to Fred's bookstore I had a notion I was being followed. Not in the way I'd come to expect, but by someone who meant me harm. I kept turning around and saw no one whose mien was any angrier than normal, upon which I realized that any reasonably intelligent assailant would make a point of wearing as bland and distant an expression as possible. I stopped at a newsstand and bought a stack of papers—the *Guardian, le Monde, Libération,* the *Herald Tribune*—and affected an air of deep engagement as I sauntered over to an outdoor table at a café and sat.

The *Herald Tribune*'s crossword was unreasonably difficult for a Tuesday, and as I drank my coffee and concentrated on the puzzle, I'm moderately embarrassed to say that I forgot all about my absurd notion about being followed. All I can say about that is that the prickly feeling on the back of my neck stopped, and by the time I got up and left, my mind was on other things (39 Down: McKinley assassin), and by the time I made it to Fred's bookstore, I was back in the world of the Venus de Milo, raring to solve her mysteries.

Fred seemed happy to see me but a wariness remained. "Hadn't called you yet," he said. "I did buy a book on screenwriting, though."

"That's great," I said. "So here's what we call in Hollywood the 'High Concept,' if you're ready to start."

"Shouldn't I be signing a contract first?"

"I don't know, why would you need to do that?"

"I don't even know how much you're going to pay me."

I shook my head. "This isn't that kind of a deal, Fred."

"Frédéric," he said.

"Okay, listen. This is what we call a spec deal. You and I write the script, I get us some meetings, and someone else gives us the money for the script."

"Us?"

"You and me. You'll get the lion's share of the script money, I'll just take a story credit. And when it gets made you'll be a producer and get a fee for that, too."

"I've got an idea. Why don't you just hire me to write the script?"

I shook my head again, hoping that Fred's naïveté was a sign of his purity as an artist and not of his being a greedy pain in the ass. "In the film business you never shell out your own money. It's unprofessional. Which doesn't mean I won't have a little money thrown your way in the meantime, it just means I don't want to be your boss. I want to collaborate."

He looked down at the floor, his mouth twisted into a petulant scowl. "It's just that I was hoping I'd be able to quit this job in order to work on the script."

"You'll be quitting the job before you know it. Now listen. I'll reimburse you for the screenwriting book, and I'll buy you dinner tonight while I pitch you the story I've cooked up."

"Sure," he said, trying hard to be cheery.

"Stop by the hotel at eight-thirty. I'll be in the bar." As I put my hand on the door I remembered the half-finished crossword I carried under my arm. "Hey, you don't happen to know who shot McKinley, do you?"

"The American president?"

"Yeah."

"Leon Czolgosz," he said, as if it were obvious.

"Spell it?" I said, pen poised over the grid. He did so, and the letters fit perfectly, providing me with a solid framework for finishing the puzzle once I got back to the hotel. "Thanks, pal."

• • •

The lovely Annick was waiting for me in the lobby, thumbing through a copy of *The New York Review of Books* and looking like an impatient young queen awaiting an underling. I stopped by her chair and cleared my throat.

"Would Her Majesty care for a refreshment in the Presidential Suite?"

Her air of cool detachment, I was pleased to see, evaporated and she beamed at me. "Absolutely."

Half an hour later she was pulling on her sweatpants and giggling about how mad her boyfriend was.

"Why, exactly, is he mad?"

"Fucking typical double standard, he wants to bang every girl he meets, but me, I'm supposed to keep myself monogamous. Fuck that."

"And how, exactly, does he know you've been unfaithful?"

She looked puzzled. "I told him."

I've never understood the compulsion to confess. To stray, of course, (this will come as no surprise to the reader at this point), but what's the advantage in talking about it afterward? I said as much to Annick and she shrugged.

"The other day when I met you and skipped the movie Bruno went anyway, and because he was mad he picked up the girl selling tickets and took her back to our apartment. I got home and found them lying there in our bed asleep, and I told him I didn't care because I'd just fucked Dr. Crandall from *Ventura County*. He didn't believe me until I showed him your picture from the park."

Jesus. "Sauce for the goose," I said in English.

"My mom was thrilled when I told her."

"You told your mother you slept with me?"

"I told her I met you. Bruno was the one who told her I slept with you. What are you doing tonight?"

"I've got a dinner meeting. Give me a call on the cell, though; it might end early." By which I meant I might be bringing Marie-Laure back to the suite.

"All right. I'll call. But I'd better not find out you're out with some other girl," she said with a smirk that might have signified anything from actual possessiveness to a wry acknowledgment of the ridiculousness of a twenty-three-year-old feeling such a thing toward a man my age. If it was some sort of possessiveness I'd have to watch myself; something in those eyes told me Annick was a girl capable of mayhem, if the circumstances were right.

• • •

Waiting downstairs for Fred, I talked for a while with the lobby bartender, who was hip enough not to let on that he knew I was an actor. I imagined a lot of celebrities came through the hotel, bigger ones than me, and there was a protocol to be followed.

Fawning was for squares, not professionals who dealt with the high and mighty on a regular basis.

He was a thickset young fellow with a brushy moustache and a nose that looked as if it had been broken more than once. Turned out he was an ex-boxer.

"I saw Tyson bite Holyfield's ear," I said.

"No shit? That was a sad moment for the sport."

"It truly was." I hadn't seen it, actually, but I'd seen Tyson fight once, and Holyfield several times. It was just something to say to keep the conversation flowing, but it stopped anyway, and I ended up watching a good chunk of an episode of *Ventura County* on the television above the bar. It was funny as always hearing Nicolas's voice coming out of my mouth, but as always I was impressed with his ability to capture my manner of speaking, my cadences and tones. In darker moments I believed he was better than me.

Onscreen Me was arguing with his half-sister, and based on Becky's hairstyle—long and braided—I estimated that the episode dated back about seven years, to a period when we'd broken up over some insensitive remark I'd made deliberately just to piss her off, and there was a real fire to our scene together: Her very real anger toward the real me spilled helplessly over into her character's anger with mine. I suddenly missed her, wished I had treated her better, wished we could spend a few weeks here together, but of course that was impossible given the number of entanglements I'd already entered into. Maybe Rome someday, where the show was reasonably popular but aired at a worse timeslot and where the general public hadn't gone apeshit over it the way the French had. Or maybe London, where it aired during the day, same as in the States, and was enjoyed only by the most depressive of shut-ins and unemployables.

Fred's arrival interrupted my reverie, and I shook his hand with unfeigned enthusiasm. With his skills as a writer and mine as an idea man we would come up with a script that would be impossible to turn down.

He ordered a beer and the bartender put down a fresh bowl of *amuse-gueules* before us, and I set about pitching the movie.

"I'm an archaeologist, somewhere down in the Mediterranean."

"So this is sort of an Indiana Jones thing?"

"No. I don't know, maybe. Just listen. I'm on a dig and I find a chunk of marble."

"Are you alone on the dig?"

"I don't know. Sure. Or maybe I've got my girlfriend with me."

"If you've already got a girlfriend then there's no love interest later on."

"True. No girlfriend then. Maybe just some students. I'm a professor."

"Like Indiana Jones."

"Or not. Maybe I'm sleeping with one of the students. Like a charming rogue."

"Okay. Or maybe you've got a girlfriend who's a bitch, and the audience wants you to find a different one."

I liked the way he thought. "Yeah, exactly. Anyway, I find this chunk of marble."

"Does it have to be marble?"

"Yes."

"Why? Because I have another idea about what he could find."

"Shoot."

"A mummy."

"No. It's not a horror movie. Try not to get distracted, okay? He finds a chunk of marble, and something about it makes him think, hmm, this is familiar. Where have I seen this particular type of marble before?"

"What type of marble is it? Do we need to research the different kinds?"

His inability to stay focused was starting to worry me. "Forget that for a second. Anyway, he digs some more and he figures it out. You want to know what he finds?"

"I guess."

I looked down the bar to make sure the bartender wasn't listening. They say execution is everything and inspiration counts for very little, but this was the sort of high concept that could get easily hijacked by the wrong sort of character. I leaned in and said quietly, "He finds a pair of arms."

"Skeletal arms?" Fred said.

"Marble arms."

"Okay. Marble arms. What happens next?"

"Don't you get it?"

"I guess I don't."

"They're the Venus de Milo's arms."

He looked blank. "That's your idea?"

"That's it."

"What else is there?"

"That's the start of the movie. Now we figure out the rest."

"There was already a movie maybe thirty years ago with Noiret and Annie Girardot about an archaeologist and a statue with a missing part."

"Jesus, really? The Venus de Milo?"

"No, it was a statue of Jupiter and they stole his leg."

"Then I don't see what the problem is."

"I didn't say there was one."

"Good." I was getting a little tired of his tendency to piss on my ideas, but in the end it was probably good to have someone playing devil's advocate.

"Did you read my book yet?"

"Haven't had the chance."

• • •

I'd phoned Marie-Laure and suggested she join us for dinner, in hopes that she would take a personal interest in the project and also that the network might pick up the tab. I was a little disappointed, then, when we arrived at the address she'd given me to find a quaint little restaurant on a street behind the arcades on the rue de Rivoli, a dark-walled place serving an old-fashioned cuisine and making the most of a nineteenth-century ambience. It was perfectly charming, mind you, the kind of place where you were likely to get a very good meal, but I'd been hoping for a sign that the network held me in somewhat higher esteem.

An outbreak of whispering erupted when I walked in the door and presented myself to the maître d', at least half a dozen diners urging their companions to turn around and look at who just walked in. I smiled and affected an air of approachable affability and winked at one plump, blushing matron as we passed her table on our way to our own, causing her to burst into a fit of giggling.

Marie-Laure was already there, and when I introduced her to Fred she frowned and cocked her head sideways, repeating his name.

"Did you write *Squirm, Baby, Squirm?*"

He appeared stunned. His novel, I gathered, hadn't garnered many sales or reviews, and this may have been the first time anyone ever recognized his name as the author thereof. "I did."

"I thought it was superb. Very provocative, particularly the sex scenes between the brother and sister."

"Thank you."

"Did you ever sell the film rights?"

"No one ever inquired."

She rolled her eyes, shook her head, and took a sip of her aperitif. "You can't wait for someone to inquire, you have to be aggressive. Who's your agent?"

"I don't have one."

"We'll have to get you one," she said, perusing the day's specials, clipped onto the plastic menu. "There's monkfish medallions tonight, it's usually good here. In fact the seafood is always good here."

"I don't believe in them, generally," Fred said, with a touch of fear in his voice.

"In monkfish medallions?" Marie-Laure said.

"Agents." I was relieved to hear him say this, because it occurred to me that an agent might fuck up our deal if he got involved too soon. Just then the waiter came with Fred's and my drinks, and Fred took a long, nervous swig of his.

"Don't be a dumbass," she said. "How much did you get for that novel?"

Fred looked as though she'd just inquired as to his sperm count, or past sexual encounters with barnyard animals. He took another swig and answered. "Five hundred euros."

Marie-Laure rolled her eyes. "My God, you need an agent more than any writer I ever met. I'll set you up with one, all right?" Fred looked to me in supplication as she turned her attention back so completely to the menu that a response didn't seem called for. The waiter, an unusually tall, white-haired specimen who would have been even taller had his neck not been bent permanently forward from years of leaning down to listen to diners, appeared tableside at this juncture to take our orders. Thick, snowy-white hairs grew from his ears, a detail that fascinated me to such an extent that I forgot completely what I'd decided to order and had to reconsult the menu.

When the waiter left, Marie-Laure finally spoke and fixed on Fred as if I weren't there. In fact, now that I thought of it, she hadn't addressed a word to me since "*Salut*."

"You have other novels?"

"One other I'm working on."

"How can you work on it while you're doing this script?"

"I can do two things at once. They're different forms."

"How many scripts have you written?"

He hesitated, but he was so intimidated by her stare that he didn't dare lie. "This is the first."

"That's good," she said, to his and my surprise. "You haven't learned any bad habits. Just get the formatting right and you'll be fine."

"You think so?"

"I know so. I read *Squirm, Baby, Squirm,* and you have an excellent sense of structure, plot, and pace. In fact when I read it I thought, this is practically filmable right off the page as it is. The part where his twin sister discovers she's pregnant with her own brother's doomed baby gave me chills."

Fred was clearly unused to such face-to-face compliments, and his face burned red. He was sweating, too, and I had the feeling Marie-Laure inspired the same reaction in him that she did in me.

"How come you didn't try to buy it for the network? Too racy?" I asked, and she turned to me as if I'd interrupted a private conversation.

"Don't be a fucking idiot. This isn't the United States, where you can't even show a tit without causing a national panic attack. It's because visually it should be a movie, for the cinema. Anyway, we don't work with the kinds of budgets where we can send a crew to Bangkok."

A timid little man wearing a bowtie approached the table holding something with both hands at chest level, and when I turned to greet him I thought he was going to faint. "Excuse me," he said, "but are you the actor who plays Dr. Crandall on *Ventura County* on the television?"

"I am," I said.

"I wonder if you'd be so kind as to inscribe this for my mother?"

He extended the object in his hands. It was a copy of the latest *Télé 7 Jours*, from whose cover I stared in my OR scrubs, grim in my determination to save some critically ill or injured soul. "How would you like me to sign it?"

"'For Eugénie,' please."

I whipped out my trusty marker and wrote it, my real name and "Dr. Crandall Taylor, MD" after that. He smiled and returned to his table, where he was dining with a well-dressed fellow several decades his junior, who gave me what seemed to me a rather resentful glance.

"Honestly," Marie-Laure said, annoyed that I'd stopped following her conversation with Fred. "I don't know how you put up with that."

"It's all right. I knew what I signed up for when I became an actor."

"But the impertinence of interrupting a private conversation . . ."

"Begging your pardon, Marie-Laure, but I was hardly part of that conversation." I gave her my famous TV glare, a visual dressing-down with one eyebrow raised in judgmental disdain. It needed to be done at this stage, lest she think me a fool or an underling to be ordered around—a delicate matter, since there really was no question that I needed her help, and rather desperately.

It did the trick. She melted immediately. "Don't be an asshole," she said. "Of course you were part of it. So tell me about your project. Who's attached so far?"

"Just me."

Fred looked panicked. I'd just admitted that, in essence, there was no project except as it existed in our heads. But I was giving Marie-Laure a shot at the ground floor; besides, she was a pro, and there'd be no fooling her.

"That's good. No one we'll have to get rid of if I come up with someone better." She took a tiny chunk of bread and nibbled thoughtfully. "Can I read the script?"

"Not yet."

"You haven't even started it, have you?"

"We have," I said, which was more or less true, since we'd been talking about it, which is half the process of writing. "But it's not ready yet."

"How long?"

I looked over at Fred. "Two weeks," I said, and those panicky eyes got a little wider.

"What's the concept?"

"I'm an archaeologist, and I find the arms of the Venus de Milo."

She nodded, lower lip protruding in a pensive manner I found very fetching. I certainly hoped I was going to take her home with me tonight. "That's good. Comedy or adventure?"

"A little of both. Of course it can be tailored to your tastes."

"No, no, suit yourselves and I'm sure it will be fine for our needs."

The meal itself (on my part, onion soup, trout meunière, a decent Alsatian Riesling, profiteroles—the sort of meal one might have ordered in the same restaurant a century earlier) was consumed without discussion of business matters, not because of any scruples or good manners on my part or that of Fred, but because Marie-Laure seemed to consider the matter closed for the time being. When the coffee came, Fred was unable to contain himself any longer.

"When do we get paid?"

Marie-Laure shrugged. "Ask him," she said, gesturing toward me. "The network is interested, but there will have to be a finished script before we can commit."

Poor Fred looked like he was going to cry.

• • •

Marie-Laure declined my invitation to return to the suite with me. "It's my husband's birthday," she said before gracing me with a perfunctory set of *bisous* and climbing into her cab. Fred had already started walking back to wherever he lived, and I was at loose ends for the rest of the evening.

I pulled my phone from my inside jacket pocket and scanned my texts (I'm from the old school; I never interrupt a dinner with friends or colleagues for phone calls or texts). To my delight, one of the messages was from Annick: "Meet me? New club: Hanoi Hilton. Afterward, yr hotel?" Beneath this was an address on a pedestrian street in the fifth, near a bookshop I used to frequent. I hopped in a cab just as someone cried out in near hysterical excitement: "Crandall!"

• • •

More of an alley than a street—I imagined that furniture delivery days must have been interesting affairs here—the street featured only two businesses, the aforementioned bookshop, closed for the night, and a nightclub whose signage featured a painting of bald, fat Brando from *Apocalypse Now*, beneath a neon sign reading, yes, HANOI HILTON. I supposed no one had consulted a trademark lawyer before opening up, and wondered whether the inevitable financial settlement with the hotel chain would leave them with enough operating capital to reopen with a new name. To the sound of earsplitting disco music I descended a narrow stone staircase of medieval construction and at the bottom arrived at a checkpoint, at which a giant of Polynesian origin stood taking the cover charge and stamping the hands of those who left.

"Fifteen."

"That includes how many drinks?" I asked.

"Drinks are extra," he said. Behind him on the walls were movie posters, both predictable—*Apocalypse Now*, *Platoon*, *The Deer Hunter*—and idiosyncratic, forgotten titles like *The Boys in Company C*, and at least one—*Hamburger Hill*—that wasn't set in Vietnam at all. As I fiddled with my wallet at a dilatory rate of speed, a grinning, dark-haired man in an expensive suit approached, his hand extended in greeting. If my guess was right, he was the owner or the manager, and I was about to save a cool fifteen euros.

"Forget it, Sammy, the doctor doesn't pay for anything around here."

Sammy looked unconvinced but waved me past the velvet rope, and my benefactor introduced himself as Mathieu as he led me to the bar. I ordered a shot and a bottle of Carlsberg as Mathieu introduced me to all and sundry—hostesses, three bartenders, several older gents whom I took to be investors, current or potential—and as we drank, any number of attractive young women approached. I signed a couple of dozen autographs, including at least five on human flesh, before things calmed down enough for Mathieu to talk.

"So what brings you here?"

"Trying to get a movie made," I said.

"No, here to the club?"

"Meeting a friend," I said. "I haven't seen her, though."

He looked across the room at Sammy, who was having some sort of problem with a group at the checkpoint. "Just a minute, I have something I want to discuss with you."

I started watching a staggeringly beautiful brunette of thirty-five or so dance with a burly twenty-year-old with blond dreadlocks and no sense of rhythm whatsoever. She looked determined to put him in his place either on the dance floor or elsewhere, and I made a mental note: If they separated, and if Annick didn't show, I was going to make a play for her.

A girl danced for the crowd in rags in a bamboo cage suspended above the dance floor, her hot pants torn in just the right way to show a tantalizing glimpse of bush and her T-shirt ripped so that most of her right breast was visible. She was, I suppose, intended to represent a female POW, perhaps one who had disguised herself as a man in order to get into the air force and fly bombing missions over Hanoi.

Nursing my beer and looking around I wondered how you got a bank to loan you the money for such a venture. Maybe I could invent some similarly off-putting idea for a drinking and dancing establishment and reinvent myself as an entrepreneur, adding "well-known impresario of the Parisian nightlife" to my CV. A serial killer–themed nightclub, maybe, with Eddie Gein–inspired human-skin masks lining the walls. Bartenders dressed as John Wayne Gacy in full clown makeup. Portraits on the walls of BTK and Ted Bundy and Richard Ramirez. (Why were all the serial killers who came to my mind American? I'm well aware that Europe and specifically France have produced any number of homicidal monsters. Maybe the theme needed to be that specific in order to interest investors.)

I had that funny, prickly feeling again that I was being watched, which of course I was, surreptitiously or openly by two thirds of the people in the club. But again this was different, that sensation of being spied on with hostile intent, and though it was almost certainly nonsense, I was nonetheless on my guard.

I finished my beer and headed for the bathroom, finding it empty. I urinated with the overwhelming yet indistinct thumping of the bass passing through the door, a reasonably good likeness of R. Lee Ermey painted on the opposite wall and visible in the mirror. Ermey reminded me a good deal of my own drill sergeant in the dawning days of my military career, and I wondered what had become of cranky old Sergeant McMillan. Probably making the retirees run drills down in Florida. I should track him down, maybe pay a visit; he was the one who taught me my first choke hold. Seeing my enthusiasm and sensing a kindred soul, he took me under his wing and instructed me in the way of the warrior. Unarmed, I was capable of killing an attacker in any of a dozen ways, a knowledge that leads paradoxically to a state of great calm via a lack of fear.

As I zipped up, the door opened and the young man with the blond dreadlocks entered, an expression of undiluted anger on his face, and called me a fucking sack of shit.

He pulled back his fist in an attempt to sucker punch me, but he was pitiably slow and I got in a good shot to his solar plexus. He dropped back against the wall, right into a painting of Tom Berenger dying in *Platoon*, and I planted my heel down hard on his metatarsals. The first blow had taken his breath away, so he didn't scream, but as he slid down to the tile flooring he certainly fucking wanted to. In my jacket pocket was a telescoping steel tactical baton my friend Byron, a cop and former advisor to the show on police matters, had given me as a gift before I left, but its use didn't seem necessary now.

"Here's the thing about dreads," I said. "They look great if you're black, but if you're a pasty blond white kid they make you look like a douchebag and a poser."

• • •

When I got back to the bar I was told Mathieu was waiting in the private salon. This was located behind a door guarded by another Polynesian, this one even bigger than Sammy, who opened up and waved me inside. Waiting for me in the luxuriously appointed room were Mathieu and the brunette my assailant had been dancing with, whom Mathieu introduced as Esmée. Not knowing whether she was attached to Mathieu, and having just been attacked by another of her admirers, I didn't press my attentions on her, but her cocked eyebrow suggested an interest in getting to know one another.

"You mentioned a movie," Mathieu said. "As it happens Esmée is an actress as well as a model."

"Is that so. I knew I'd seen you before," I said, though this wasn't the case.

"Mostly commercials. A small part in a Dutch film last year."

"Her husband is one of the investors here. Is your film funded yet?"

"Not completely. We're still looking for co-producers."

Esmée smiled, and I could easily imagine that face on screen. Her head was large in proportion to her body, and if that sounds like a backward compliment, it isn't. Head-to-body ratio is one of the key elements of stardom, determining how a person photographs. Look back at the great stars of twentieth-century cinema: Bogart, Bette Davis, Gabin, Gable—all had enormous heads in relation to their bodies. It's no different in modern times: Hoffman, Depardieu, Julia Roberts, Jackie Chan. Picture Philippe Noiret with his head slightly smaller, and suddenly he's your neighborhood grocer, or trash collector. Without his massive head threatening to capsize his tiny body every time he takes a step, Tom Cruise is the guy who tears the tickets at the movie theater, not the giant on the screen.

"As it happens my husband is looking for a project to fund, something I could be in."

"Something that might feature the club as well. Is there room for a nightclub scene?"

"Absolutely, it'll fit right in. I'm meeting with the writer in the morning."

"Splendid. Maybe you can bring him along tomorrow night? The place should be a bit more lively. In the meantime, anything you want from the bar is on the house."

The door opened and the blond kid with dreadlocks stepped inside. He looked chastened, though not necessarily by me. Esmée's expression grew stern.

"Are you ready to take me home now?" she asked. No, let me amend that; though posed in the form of a question, it was nonetheless a command. She turned to me, all smiles again. "Let me introduce my stepson, Bruno."

• • •

It was around three in the morning when I got out of the taxi in front of the hotel, and for once there was no one passing on the sidewalk to stop and point. The lobby was nearly empty, and the man at the reception showed no sign of recognition as he handed me my key and wished me a pleasant night's sleep. As I climbed into bed, by myself for once, I almost felt as though I were someone else.

MERCREDI, QUATRE MAI

AS A YOUNG MAN I CARRIED AROUND A GREAT deal of anger, and I used to be a brawler. Not the kind I am now, where somebody else starts the thing and I finish it, but the kind who looks for trouble and starts it when there's none to be found. When I was seventeen years old I got into a fight over a girl and put the other guy into the hospital with a broken clavicle. When I came before the judge for sentencing he offered me a choice, much like the choice the army gave me later on: I could go to jail for a year and a half, or I could enlist. What the hell, I thought, the army sounded like a good way to bust some heads, and I joined up. I did so well in Basic Training they kicked me upstairs, and I kept on acing every test they gave me until I got into U.S. Army Special Forces. The Green Berets.

Once in, I continued to outperform all my peers intellectually and physically. I'd finally found something I was good at, better than anybody else around me. I was born to be a warrior.

The trouble was, I kept that anger coiled in me like a spring, and all the training was doing was wrapping that spring tighter and tighter. I hadn't found a way to let it out, and then one day, having been taught a couple of dozen ways to kill a man with my bare hands, an opportunity for release presented itself while I was buying a six-pack of beer.

A young enlisted man was shopping with his doughy, sad-looking wife and two kids. Despite the wear and tear visible on her face, she was no more than twenty-five and retained sad vestiges of a genuine beauty lost to disappointment, early motherhood, and life on an army base. One of the few advantages for family men in the armed services is the base PX, where prices are a fraction of what they are in civilian grocery stores, but this guy wasn't happy about the bargains to be had; he was bitching and moaning to his wife about the amount of food she was loading into their cart. One of the kids, a boy of about six with a blond crewcut bleached by the sun, grabbed a package of potato chips from the shelf and tore it open. The dad, a corporal, saw this and yanked his son by the arm and, while the kid was still in midair, smacked him across the face.

There's a protocol to be followed in these cases. You alert the MPs, you get witnesses, you deal with it through the proper channels. What you don't do is go all kung fu on the poor unsuspecting bastard, break both his arms and legs and put a crack in his skull so hard he'll never quite think right again. All of which, without really considering the consequences or the logic of it, is what I did to that poor cracker son of a bitch, right there in front of his wife and kids, who looked upon me not as their rescuer but as an assailant, a turn of events which, though predictable and quite understandable, made me sad.

In the brig I had some time to think it over. I was more than a little bit frightened by what I'd done, particularly by the speed with which my rage had overtaken me, and after some words with my commanding officer and with an army shrink I came to the conclusion that maybe a little bit of psychiatric work might be in order. My CO was a standup guy, and though he couldn't pull enough strings to keep me in the unit (this was during peacetime—there's no way today's U.S. military would have kicked me out), he did manage to get me the option of a discharge instead of prison time.

Once out, I thought about pursuing therapy, but instead I managed to lie my way through the application process well enough to find myself accepted into Southwest Minnesota State University, where I promptly signed up for a theater course on the assumption that this would be where the good-looking girls were.

And the assumption wasn't wrong. The thing was, though, I discovered that there was something else I was really good at. Before long I was the star of the department, was stringing along a half-dozen nubile beauties, and had discovered that acting was for me a means of controlling my anger as well as a path to self-knowledge. Since that time, I have never instigated a fight (though I've never run from one, either).

• • •

I had an interview and photo shoot scheduled with *Télérama* at eleven o'clock at the Musée Rodin. I had a reputation in the press for being an intellectual, at least by the standards of television actors, and the editors thought it would be a good visual joke to get me posing beneath *The Thinker.* The joke was probably on me—God knows, a few years of covering television would have made me hate the medium and everyone involved in it—but press was press, and I had a good working relationship with the reporter. We spent half an hour on the photos and then hunkered down in the restaurant in the garden for the interview.

Here I was at a loss: to mention the movie or not? Bad luck to talk about a project too early, certainly, but *Télérama* has a lot of readers, including no small number in the industry, and a casual allusion to the thing might cause some ears to prick up. And of course the film was about a piece of sculpture, and here we were amidst one of the great sculpture collections of the world.

"So what brings you back to Paris? Just a vacation, promoting the show?" my interlocutor asked.

"A little of both," I said, cagey. Then I thought, what the hell. Let's make this thing happen. "Truth to tell, I'm in the early stages of a film project, a Franco-American coproduction."

"You don't say. Who's attached?"

"There's a brilliant script by a young French novelist named Frédéric LaForge, he wrote a terrific book called *Squirm, Baby, Squirm*, and we've been working on getting the deals finalized."

"What's it about?"

"All I can say is that it's about an archaeologist who makes an incredible discovery." It sounded lame and incomplete as I said it, but Henri seemed very interested.

"That's great. Is the network involved?"

"It's not official yet, so don't quote me, but it's looking good."

• • •

If I'm going to be talking up Fred's book, I thought, I'd better read the damned thing, so I spent a good chunk of the afternoon absorbing it in the day room of the suite. It was well written—the kid could sling a phrase with the best of them, no question—but it was beyond the pale in terms of content. The main character, Jim, is so promiscuous and amoral that it was hard for me to picture my soft-spoken, mild-mannered new friend and collaborator as his creator. In the book's Thai section, for example, Jim fucks eighteen prostitutes, nine of them underage and four of them boys. Each of the prostitutes is described in detail, along with those of Jim's couplings with him or her, and by the end of that part of the book he's actively seeking those who show the most advanced signs of disease:

> *The pathetic wraith struggling beneath me, her breath stinking of her own impending demise, wheezed and rattled as though the withered flesh on her meager frame were insufficient to keep her dried bones from cracking together with each thrust; by the time old Thanatos finally arrived to claim his due from her I would be back in France, an enthusiastic vessel of her contagion.*

When he leaves Thailand and returns to France he lives a life of outward bourgeois respectability, faithfully attending mass as an almost daily communicant and reveling in the blasphemy of receiving the host under false pretenses, his confessions consisting of trivial lies. He tends to his family's business and maintains an air of conservative respectability, all the while diligently attempting to infect his sister with a lethal venereal disease (the novel is set in the 1990s, before the medicinal cocktails that have prolonged so many lives in the West). The high point of his depravity comes when he blackmails a pharmacist friend into confecting a placebo pill in the shape and color of his sister's birth control pills, which he then substitutes for the real thing.

> *The replacement of the changeling pills into their circular dispenser was a more complicated and time-consuming affair than I'd imagined, but the task was completed before Valerie returned from her ballet lesson. My extensive readings on the subject notwithstanding, and despite my intimate familiarity with the timing of her menses, I couldn't determine her precise date of ovulation without arousing suspicion, and so*

I determined to make love to her every day until such time as I could be certain I'd infected her with an additional unwelcome passenger to accompany the first.

My God. I'd assumed I was working with an eccentric, because let's face it, the guy was a writer and they're all a little goofy, but this one was out of his fucking mind. Shaking hands with him the next time we met would be fraught with bacteriological worries.

Still, I couldn't deny that the book had a certain narrative pull to it, and not simply because of the ghastliness of its subject matter and the appalling depravity of its central character. Marie-Laure was right, Fred really did have the knack for structure and character and all the other things that make a screenplay filmable. And of course I'd be there to make sure the archaeologist didn't end up fucking his sister or some mummy he dug up in the desert, so where was the harm?

There was a knock at the door and I put the book down, unsure of whether I'd have the stomach to pick it up later. Outside stood a bellman with a large gift basket from Fouquet's wrapped in cellophane. After he put it on the coffee table I signed for it, tipped him ten euros, and closed the door. In the basket was an assortment of fine cheeses and two bottles of champagne, themselves wrapped in orange cellophane: Louis Roederer Cristal Brut, '99. I didn't recognize the label, but I had a strong sensation that it wasn't cheap.

The card attached read simply

FROM ESMÉE

LOOK FORWARD TO WORKING WITH YOU

Mixed feelings abounded. Spectacular creature that Esmée was, I had high hopes for her husband's money, and any entanglements would have to proceed with the greatest of delicacy and tact. Not that the gift of a couple of bottles of expensive booze necessarily indicated any inclinations toward adultery, but I couldn't help noticing that the basket also contained two champagne flutes, not one.

JEUDI, CINQ MAI

CROSSING THE LUXEMBOURG GARDENS I stopped to watch the little children pushing their toy sailboats in the fountain. There weren't many adults around and those present showed no interest in me, which for once came as a relief rather than a disappointment or a blow to my ego. A boy of about eight with oddly wide-set eyes frowned at me in a puzzled way as though trying to place me; he elbowed the frail lad next to him, who looked at me and shrugged, indifferent, and they both turned their attention back to their boats, relaxed and happy in a way I only dimly remembered from my own benighted, violent childhood. The breeze that billowed in those toy sails was cool on my forehead, and I wandered over to a bench in the shade and opened up the *Herald Tribune* to the crossword.

I was well into it when to my annoyance I felt my phone vibrating in my trouser pocket. The display identified the caller as my agent, and I came very close to not answering, but there was always the off chance he had something interesting, so I picked up.

"Hello, Bunny," I said.

"Don't call me that."

"What's up, Ted?"

He heaved a long sigh. "You're up for a part on *Blindsided*. Guest shot with potential follow-ups."

"What's *Blindsided*? I never heard of it."

"It's a detective who's blinded in an accident, and afterward she can see who did that week's crime."

"She sees it? Thought she was blind."

"She sees it in her mind, okay?"

"Network or cable?"

"Network."

"So even if my character gets to fuck the star, it'll all be off-screen. Who's the detective?"

"Mary Margaret Casterlin. Jesus, even if you don't read the trades you should at least watch television so you know this stuff."

"Really? She's doing TV?"

"Hadn't done a feature in four years when she got the offer. And she's a client, which is how I got the strings pulled to get you the offer. So you need to be back here in a week."

I thought about it. Mary Margaret Casterlin was a rare beauty and a truly gifted actress, and despite the fact that she was well known to be happily married to a real estate mogul from Santa Barbara and mother to a litter of four charming moppets, she was also strongly reputed to be an adherent of the "eatin' ain't cheatin'" school of thought on marital fidelity, particularly when on location away from home for more than a night or two. My old pal Dan Needles had shot a movie of Mary Margaret's a few years back, a romantic comedy set in San Francisco, and when she discovered that her co-star (no, I won't name him) was uninterested in the ladies except when the paparazzi were around, she approached

Dan for a bit of commiseration. Mary Margaret spent the next five weeks sucking Dan's cock in her trailer, in his trailer, in the grip truck, and twice on sets closed for the night. He spoke of those blowjobs with genuine awe and said that even a garden-variety handjob from her was better than full-blown intercourse with most women. And though in all that time he never gave up hope that she would acquiesce and allow him entry into her pussy, every makeout session ended in the same manner, with him ejaculating down her throat (or, as indicated, onto the back of her hand).

"I just happen to think that's for marriage only," she told him once when he pressed her about her reasons for refusing normal intercourse with him. "I would never do that to my husband."

So there was that prospect to consider. Plus there was the fact that the role might be recurring, which might lead to something regular on another show, which might eventually get me my own show, and by that I mean a prime-time gig, not another fucking daytime soap. There was a lot to be said for the deal.

And yet.

"I can't do it, Ted."

"What the fuck do you mean you can't do it?"

"I've got a project I'm working on over here at the moment. A lead role."

"In what?"

"It's too soon to talk about it."

"Too soon? I'm your fucking agent, for Christ's sake."

"I'm developing it myself, Bunny."

I could hear him slowly exhaling on the other end of the line. I was sure his face was getting red, and equally sure that some subordinate was going to get verbally reamed as soon as I hung up.

"Listen up. I stuck my neck out with another client to get you this gig. You make damn sure you're back here in a week."

"Goodbye, Bunny." I hung up, and as soon as I did I felt a little guilty about that last "Bunny," which for all I knew might cause him to hemorrhage. An old lover of his, a set designer named Giorgio, kept referring to Ted as "Bunny" at a dinner party, and ever since I've been tormenting him with it.

Sometimes, when I really think about it, I can be a bit of an asshole.

VENDREDI, SIX MAI

THE MEETING AT THE NETWORK WAS INFORMAL; besides Fred and me there was just Marie-Laure, Jean-Pierre, and some assistant-level note-takers. I mentioned Esmée, and Marie-Laure nodded.

"She was in a Dutch film last year. Not a bad performance for a model. What's your angle?"

I squirmed a bit, certain that the real question being asked was "Are you planning to fuck her?" But I pressed on, outwardly oblivious. "Her husband has a lot of money, and he'd like to see her in a leading role. We could be talking about a theatrical release, if he sees the project as worth her time and his money."

Jean-Pierre nodded. "We could make that happen, if the money's there."

"How did you meet her?" Marie-Laure asked.

"Her husband owns a nightclub in the fifth I'm going back there tonight, if you want to join me."

"I'm having dinner with my husband and his boss. We should be done by midnight, write down the address."

One of the assistants raised her hand. I called on her by raising both eyebrows inquisitively.

"What's her role?"

I looked over at Fred, and so did the rest of the attendees. "What?" he said, looking and sounding slightly panicked. "You're asking me?"

"Fred's unaccustomed to these kinds of meetings. Being a novelist he's used to keeping his counsel until the work is completed. Esmée's character would be a sort of femme fatale, who's orchestrating things behind the scenes. We're even toying with the idea of having her be the one who planted the arms where Troy finds them."

"Who's Troy?" Jean-Pierre asked.

"That's my character."

"Don't be a fuckhead," Marie-Laure said. "That's a number, not a name. Change it. I want you two to get cracking and get me a synopsis I can show the brass. I'd also like you to start the script itself, so we can start breaking it down and sending it around to other funding entities."

"Will do," I said, and as Fred sat there looking stunned I wrote down the address of the Hanoi Hilton and handed it to Marie-Laure, who glared down at the slip of paper as though it were an enemy to be vanquished.

• • •

Annick showed up at the hotel unannounced again, and though I chided her for it I was actually glad to see her. I also took her to task for failing to show up last night at the club.

"What club?" she said.

"You sent me a text."

"I did no such thing."

"It was from your number."

"Oh, my God." She looked stricken. "Bruno."

Bruno. Where had I heard that name in the last day or two? "Who's that?"

"My boyfriend. He took my phone, the dirty fucker."

Now I remembered Bruno. "He's not a stupid-looking white kid with long blond dreadlocks, is he?"

"Not anymore. He cut them off this morning."

"Why?"

"I don't know. He was upset, he got home really late last night."

The thing was getting more complicated than I liked. I made a solemn vow to myself that for the rest of the trip I was going to be faithful to Marie-Laure, at least to the degree of staying away from any woman having anything to do with young Bruno.

Just as soon as I finished up with Annick. One last time; after all, it would have been rude to kick her out.

SAMEDI, SEPT MAI

I STOPPED BY FRED'S APARTMENT ON THE WAY to the Hanoi Hilton and it was—I'm not kidding—smaller than my bathroom at home. It was on the sixth floor of a building in the tenth, a building whose stairwell smelled overpoweringly of a hundred years' worth of dust and ammonia, whose railing rattled and creaked as I mounted the floors. Two elderly women were screaming threatening obscenities at one another through the door of the apartment at the end of the hallway as I knocked on his door, and when he opened it I was shocked at the size of it.

"Hey," he said. He pointed at the table, where an old electric typewriter sat. "Take a seat."

I couldn't help but notice that there was only one chair. "Where are you going to sit?"

"I know a place I can get another chair when we work."

"You know what, this is awfully small and I get a little claustrophobic. Why don't we work back at the hotel?"

He gave me a blank look, not sure whether to be hurt or not. "This is where I do all my work," he said.

"Do you work on a typewriter?"

He nodded. "When I can. I hate using the computer." At that moment the screaming started up again, and even through the closed door every filthy syllable was completely clear.

I nodded in the direction of the shouting. "That ever get a little distracting?"

"Sometimes. They're a mother and daughter. They're at it every day since I moved in."

Scanning the apartment, I saw no bed. "Where do you sleep?"

He pointed to a chest of drawers, atop which lay a pair of blankets and a pillow. "I bed down on the floor. It's good for your back."

"And what do the ladies make of that?"

Baffled, he jerked his thumb in the direction of the termagants down the hall. "Those two?"

"No, I mean what happens when you meet a girl and bring her home and she finds out you're planning to fuck her on the floor?"

"Oh." He shrugged, looking as sad as I'd seen anyone look in a while. "Doesn't happen very often anymore."

"Why not?"

"They're all after guys with money and good jobs. Nice apartments. Cars. I work in a bookstore and I sleep on the floor."

"Bullshit, man. You've given up."

"Easy for you to say. You're a big TV star, all you have to say is 'Hello' and bang, she's going home with you."

"You're a famous novelist."

"Famous? My book sold less than five thousand copies."

"Marie-Laure read it."

"She's a statistical anomaly."

"Look, Fred. When's the last time you got laid?"

"A year ago."

"You haven't been laid in a year? What kind of Frenchman are you?" He looked like he was about to cry, so I dropped that particular line of argument. "How'd it happen the last time?"

"I was married to her." His expression got a notch sadder.

"So that's it. You were married for a while and forgot how to pick up women. It happens. I guarantee I'm going to get you laid before we get any further with this project."

"It doesn't matter."

I shook my head. "It does matter. At the risk of opening up a wound, why'd you get divorced?"

He stared at the bare wooden floor, its ancient varnish mostly worn away. "Because I found out she was fucking my best friend, that's why."

"Ah. Listen, here's what we're going to do. You know that little blond assistant of Marie-Laure's?"

"Not exactly, apart from having been at that meeting today."

"Good enough. She's coming along tonight, and I've got five euros that says she's going to take you back to her place at the end of the night."

"I don't even know her. And she's young."

"Young is good, Fred, not bad."

"I mean she's probably into all kinds of terrible youth culture. And she'll probably hate my book. Who knows if she even reads, working in television?"

"Fred," I said, straining to keep the exasperation out of my voice, "you're not marrying her tonight. You're going to attempt to insert your penis into her vagina and then remove it again, repeating the process until such time as you achieve a reasonably satisfying orgasm. I will attempt to encourage her to allow you to do this. After that if you're both of a mind to do so, you can try it again. If not, you'll fuck some other woman. Okay?"

He answered with a joyless, resigned shrug. "Let's go."

Heading for the stairs, I was terrified to hear the door to the old ladies' apartment open. I turned to face a pair of sweetly smiling old biddies, one considerably older than the other.

"Good evening, M. LaForge," they said in unison. The older one squinted at me and said, "You look just like that doctor on the television."

The younger pointed at Fred and informed me that M. LaForge was a celebrated writer. "Author of a novel."

Both of them had those sweet, high-pitched voices that older French ladies get. Fred bid them good evening with what seemed genuine fondness, and we descended at a great clip as they made their way down, step by grueling step. I wondered where they were going at nine in the evening; off to feed strychnine to the pigeons, perhaps, or to some poor trusting clochard sleeping under a bridge. In any case I felt certain that they were safer than anyone having the misfortune of running across them under cover of darkness.

• • •

We took a cab to a Chinese place near Les Halles where Fred used to eat with his wife. There were the usual cheap wall hangings and paper lanterns, Chinese pop music playing quietly over the PA, and waitresses in slit silk dresses, one of whom was a tall, slender thing with very nice legs. She found it impossible to address me directly and looked at Fred while I gave my order. When she left I watched her walk away, an impossibly slinky gait that gave me a little boner there under the table.

"So your best friend banged your old lady," I said, breaking my own spell, not really intending to say anything mean. It just came out that way.

He nodded. "He was a friend of mine, and a colleague. He was at the wedding, even. And I came home one day and heard my wife having a big, loud orgasm."

"You heard it?"

"She's a screamer."

"So how did you know she wasn't masturbating?"

"I snuck upstairs and stood by the door and I heard the bedsprings creaking, heard him calling her a dirty slut, heard her coming louder than I'd ever heard before."

"Jeez. I hope you broke his fucking legs."

He was shocked. "Of course not."

"I would have," I said, realizing even as I said it that I probably wasn't a prime example of a well-adjusted adult.

"We used to come here once every couple of weeks." He looked around. "Haven't been here since. I thought I'd feel bad, but I don't."

• • •

The Hanoi Hilton was a real clusterfuck when we got there around eleven-thirty. When Sammy the bouncer saw us standing at the top of the stairs with twenty or more people ahead of us he barked at the crowd to make way for a VIP, and for a second I thought the scene might turn ugly, but the whispers and pointing amongst those awaiting entry were excited rather than angry; the chance to rub shoulders with celebrities apparently trumped the unfairness of it. Sammy nodded at me as we passed and jerked his thumb toward the bar, where the assembled crowd parted like the Red Sea making way for Moses, people touching me on the shoulders and arms as though I could cure whatever it was that made them want to come to a place like this and pay double for watery drinks and damage their hearing to the tune of twenty-year-old disco riffs, probably not even getting laid in the bargain. The bartender handed us our comped drinks and gestured with a sideways nod toward the VIP salon, pressing a button as he did so. The door to the salon opened, and Sammy's cousin, wearing shades and an earpiece, gestured us inside as the crowd at the bar gawked.

To my surprise Marie-Laure was already there, along with the production assistant—Clarice? Félice?—I'd promised Fred he could sleep with. Marie-Laure's skirt just about came up to the crack of her ass, and the way she kept crossing and uncrossing her legs made me wonder whether she was wearing underwear or not. Esmée strode toward me and gave me the *bise*—four—and Mathieu shook my hand.

"We've been discussing your project," Esmée said. "It's fascinating. How ever did you get the idea?"

"Standing in front of the old girl and trying to picture what the arms would have looked like."

"Did you get the basket?"

"I did. I have to admit I haven't cracked open the champagne yet."

A simultaneous and brief look of anticipation crossed the faces of Marie-Laure and Esmée and, I was interested to note, that of the production assistant as well, a look that I hoped had escaped poor Fred's notice. This was unlikely, because he was staring at the poor girl with the intensity a baby gives its mother when it's sure she's about to leave the room.

"How do you find the hotel?" Esmée asked.

"Delightful," I said.

"But it must be terribly expensive."

"True enough. I really ought to look into renting something."

Esmée pressed her hand flat to her sternum. "You know, I just had a thought," she said in a way that made me certain she'd had the thought well before I arrived. "I have an apartment in the sixth, not far from here at all. It's furnished and unoccupied; the tenant left last month."

Knowing full well she was going to let me stay there for free, I played along. "That sounds ideal. What do you think per month?"

"I wouldn't dream of letting you pay. You're such a delight for even considering me for the role."

I looked over at Marie-Laure, whose face was the very picture of equanimity and indifference, and I knew she was seething. She loathed Esmée, and it didn't look like there was going to be any way to avoid the two of them working together.

As we discussed the specifics of the arrangement I glanced at Fred, who was still staring at the assistant (I really was going to have to learn her name once and for all), while she studiously ignored him. I sidled over to him as Esmée, Marie-Laure, and the object of Fred's affections huddled to discuss whether or not they should get out onto the disco floor and boogie down. Mathieu was leaning against a wall painting of Christopher Walken's exploding head, reading a comic book.

"Listen, Fred, you can't just stare at her all night. Go over and sit with her. Ask her to dance. What you're doing right now is giving her the creeps. Hell, it's giving me the creeps."

"Oh." He stared at his feet.

"When's the last time you courted a woman?"

"That was my wife. Eight, nine years."

"Were you better at it then than you are now?"

"Not really. My wife was pretty aggressive."

I turned to the assembly and announced that I was going to dance.

• • •

That girl in the cage was dressed even more skimpily than before, and I swear this time I saw a glistening flash of vulva through those raggedy shorts. I started off dancing with Esmée, while Fred took Marie-Laure for a partner and Mathieu shook it with the assistant. Esmée had a most disconcerting way of staring deep into my eyes while we danced, a look so fraught with implications I couldn't help but think that moving into her empty place was going to be a mistake. I started a silent mantra: *Her husband is going to help finance the movie. Her husband is going to help finance the movie. Her husband—*

But then I saw the way those hips moved and I didn't care about the movie at all.

When the song changed I danced with the assistant. I would have sung Fred's praises, but she seemed completely lost in the music, transported and almost unaware of my presence. I took careful stock of her with the intention of helping Fred: She was young, no more than twenty-five, she was ambitious (I thought), she was a long way from home (her accent suggested the Côte d'Azur), she was quite pretty (prettier than I'd noticed, previously, which may not have boded well for poor Fred), and she was quite a graceful dancer. She also had very long legs.

Shit. Having convinced my friend that he should make an effort to sleep with her, and him having taken the idea quite seriously, I found myself in the uncomfortable position of wanting to fuck her myself. Another mantra: *She's Marie-Laure's assistant. She's Marie-Laure's assistant. She's Marie-Laure's—*

The music changed again and I found myself dancing with a frankly chilly Marie-Laure. I was under no illusion that her anger stemmed from any particular attachment to me; it was the presence of a competitor, one who might be getting the upper hand pure and simple. She refused to look me in the eye, and I really hoped that she was going to agree to come back to the suite with me tonight, because that kind of angry sex is really better than any other kind.

DIMANCHE, HUIT MAI

SHE DID COME BACK WITH ME AROUND 3:00 AM, and she confirmed my hunch that the bottles of champagne that Esmée had sent were expensive, even more so than I'd guessed. We drank half of one bottle along with some of the cheese from the basket, then got up to some of that grudgefucking I'd been looking forward to. Afterward, lying on the floor naked, we polished off the rest of the bottle

"Doesn't your husband object to these nights when you don't come home?" I asked her.

"It's not that kind of marriage." She stretched out a long leg and stared down it as if down the barrel of a sniper's rifle. "You be careful with that Esmée. I did a little checking up, and her marriage isn't that kind."

"Meaning?"

"Meaning her husband is the kind who'd object strenuously if she strayed."

"I don't picture her as the type that strays."

Marie-Laure snorted at me. "Don't be a shit-for-brains. I saw the look she was giving you all night. So did Mathieu, who, I would remind you, works for her husband."

"Mathieu's his partner, strictly speaking."

"Don't be a dumbass. He's pure front, a manager posing as an owner. All I'm saying is if you fuck her, you'd better be damned careful."

"You hadn't struck me as the jealous type before," I said with my famous, teasing TV smirk.

"Don't be fucking stupid, I don't care who you fuck when I'm not around. I'm concerned as a friend and more importantly as a business associate with a professional stake in your remaining aboveground."

"Thanks," I said.

"Don't be a moron. You know what I mean. I think moving into that apartment of hers is asking for trouble."

"I'll take it into consideration."

• • •

Next morning over breakfast I decided it would be a good idea to break it off with Annick. Bruno had already given a violent demonstration of his jealousy, and since I was entering into a business arrangement with his stepmother I thought it best to simplify the relationship. Especially given the fact that said stepmother seemed to have some sort of hold over him that went beyond the usual stepmother/stepson oedipal crisis. Marie-Laure's warning about Esmée seemed somehow more plausible in the light of the morning, and the memory of the previous night's frolics made me wonder why I needed any woman besides Marie-Laure. Besides, it wasn't as though there weren't a thousand—ten thousand—other, equally attractive women in Paris who'd be delighted to sleep with a TV star.

• • •

In the early afternoon I packed my bags and checked out of the suite. Esmée was waiting for me with a car and driver, and in the backseat as we headed toward the Left Bank we talked about the movie.

"What's my character like?"

"That's an interesting question," I said, and it was, since I hadn't given it much thought other than that she should be pretty and have large breasts, neither of which would be much of a stretch for Esmée. "Fred and I are still hashing it out, really, so of course your input would be very helpful."

"Really?" she said, pressing her palm to her sternum again in that familiar gesture of hers. "I'm so flattered."

"Fred and I both find that it's easier to write a character when you've already got an actor in mind."

She seemed genuinely excited by the prospect of getting to design her own character. She touched the tips of her fingers to the bridge of her nose and squinted. "I'm wondering if maybe she starts out not as the love interest but as a villain. Then later on they fall in love."

"That's an interesting idea," I said. It was better than nothing, anyway, and I pulled out my iPhone and started writing it down.

"What if she's there to steal the arms for some megalomaniac art collector?"

"Huh," I said, pretending to consider it, even though it made no sense. "What would an art collector want with just the arms?"

She shrugged. "He's a megalomaniac billionaire. Who knows? I'm just saying, think about these big art heists. Somebody steals a Monet, he can't exactly walk into the Maison Drouot and sell it, can he? So someone's hired him to steal it."

"You're right, it doesn't compute. Why hire someone to steal something you can't turn around and sell? What's the point?"

"The point is, you get to own something valuable and rare, and nobody else gets to have it."

"I can't believe there's anybody like that, willing to spend that kind of dough just to be an asshole."

She smiled a little bit, an enigmatic expression worthy of the *Mona Lisa*. "Believe it. When I know you better I'll tell you some stories about the very rich."

When we pulled up in front of the building, Esmée and I got out, and when I started for the trunk to get my bags she waved me off. "Denis will get the bags. Come on up, I'll let you in and give you the tour."

• • •

The place was huge and furnished with expensive new furniture, and for contrast on the walls were paintings ranging from the seventeenth to the early twentieth centuries. At first glance I thought I identified a small Watteau and one of Degas's last, small flower paintings, and though the collection had a sort of weird eclecticism to it, somehow the pieces all worked together to suggest a singular sensibility. I thought back to what she'd said about megalomaniac art collectors and got a little nervous about la Sûreté bursting in with guns drawn to retrieve them for their rightful owners while I slept.

Denis brought my bags inside, and Esmée, having forbidden me to hand him a gratuity on the grounds that I was her guest, told him to wait in the car. I'd slip him twenty at some later date, I told myself, when she wasn't around.

"Now, my darling, would you like me to send him on his way?"

I raised an eyebrow. "I'm afraid I'm not sure what you mean."

"Cut the shit. Do you want me to stay?"

"I'd love for you to. But I think with your husband as a potential backer for the movie we should be careful . . ."

"The hell with my husband. He's in New York for five days."

"Aren't you afraid Denis will turn you in?"

"Denis works for me."

It was all sounding really good. But I didn't know enough about her husband, or about Denis, to blithely assume that they weren't in league behind Esmée's back.

And yet there she was before me, pouting slightly, moist red lips separating to reveal her tongue gliding between her barely separated upper and lower teeth, chest thrust forward to accentuate that lovely rack, eyes half shut in lustful anticipation. . . .

What the fuck. You only die once. "Yeah, send him on his way."

• • •

Having slept with a lot of actresses—probably more of them, in fact, than women who weren't—I can state unequivocally that there is no correlation between beauty and skill in the sack. Some of the homeliest women are mind-bendingly great in bed, and some of the most stunning beauties just lie there and act like they're thinking about what's on TV later that night. In fact I'd got to the point where I half-expected a bad lay from the real knockouts.

The joke was on me. Esmée knew tricks I'd never heard of, let alone tried. She explained to me exercises she did daily, similar to the ones pregnant women use to prepare for childbirth, tricks she'd learned from her yoga instructors, tips she'd paid to learn from thousand-euro-a-night call girls. Her cunt, her mouth, her asshole—the first entry into each was like the first time Adam fucked Eve (or, if you're of a more secular bent, the first time some amphibian said, hey, instead of me ejaculating into the water after you lay the eggs, how about if I stick this thing into that pretty little cloaca of yours?).

Jesus H. Christ. Now that I knew what I knew, I wouldn't blame her husband for killing me. Shit, if I were him, I'd kill me.

LUNDI, NEUF MAI

ONCE AGAIN, THE CROSSWORD EDITOR WAS fucking with me. It was only Monday, theoretically the week's easiest puzzle, but this one was driving me nuts. The crux of the problem was 17 Across, "*Christ at Emmaus* forger." Eleven letters and the last one was an *n*. I could have Googled "*Christ at Emmaus*" and "forgery" on the iPhone, but that was a move I reserved for desperation. Meanwhile the bottom half of the puzzle was mostly filled in, the morning was pleasant, and the crowd on the sidewalk perfect: Passersby waved, smiled, jostled one another at the sight of me, and several of them took pictures, but they all respected the fact that I was sitting there, drinking my coffee and working the crossword puzzle.

I wasn't quite finished when Fred joined me—17 Across was still unanswered, though I had a *v* at the beginning and a *g* in the middle. Fred ordered coffee and a *pain au chocolat* and inquired as to my well-being.

"Superb, my friend, just superb." I took a sip of my coffee, noted that it was almost too cool to drink, and swigged it down. I felt so good I was compelled to share the secret. "I fucked our leading lady yesterday."

"Is that wise?" he asked.

"No, probably not. But I'm not sorry. That woman is amazing, and it has nothing to do with her looks."

He looked skeptical on that last point.

"All right, partially her looks, but damn, she's got some skills that would put Venus herself to shame. To hew to our story's theme, if you like."

"What about her rich husband? He hasn't even agreed to do this yet, and you're doing things that are going to make him pull the plug."

"If he finds out about it, it won't be a question of pulling the plug, more like pulling the trigger. Both barrels aimed at me."

"Great. No budget and a dead star."

The waiter came and gloomy Fred ripped off an end of the bread. It looked so good, the chocolate so moist, that I asked the waiter to bring one for me along with another double espresso.

"Say, Fred, who forged *Christ at Emmaus*? Starts with a *v,* ends with an *n*. Eleven letters."

"Van Meegeren."

I counted out the letters and they fit. "Thank you, sir. You're a gentleman and a scholar. What's *Christ at Emmaus*, anyway?"

"It's a biblical scene. He painted it as a Vermeer, and he had such a success with it he painted a bunch more. They all looked like shit, if you ask me."

"Maybe we should put a forger into the script."

I had annoyed him. He sighed and looked down the street, exasperated. "To what end?"

"I don't know. Just throwing ideas out there." He didn't look placated, so I changed the subject. "Say, how'd you do with Marie-Laure's assistant the other night?"

"Nothing happened. I'm ten years older than she is, anyway."

"Who cares? Listen, you need to get laid soon. It'll change your outlook on life."

"Did you ever read *Notes from Underground*? Dostoyevsky?"

"A long time ago. That's a book, it's no way to live. Feeling sorry for yourself is bullshit."

We didn't get much more accomplished that morning, and I was afraid that unless Fred started getting some pussy in his diet he was going to sink further and further into moroseness and become useless to me. I didn't want to break in another writer, and I was confident Fred and I could hash out something decent.

• • •

A day later I got an e-mail from a friend in L.A. letting me know that Ginny DeKalb was on her way to Paris. He meant it as a warning, but I didn't take it as such. As soon as I heard I logged on to her website, looked at some of her most recent pornos, and found her looking good indeed. She'd let our mutual friend know that she intended to look me up, and I certainly intended to let her do that.

"She's getting wackier and wackier," the e-mail read, "and that fuckup husband is causing her trouble right and left. So beware."

I wrote him back: "The day I need to beware of a lady like Ginny, my friend, is the day they plant me in the ground."

In that same batch was an e-mail from my agent, prevailing upon me in the most urgent terms to get my ass back to L.A. and do the guest shot on *Blindsided*. They really wanted me for it, and did I have any idea how fucking hard he'd worked to get it for me?

"Dear Bunny," I replied, "Thanks so much for your efforts but I'm really committed to this French project." Why in God's name would I want to give up fame, virtually unlimited pussy, and a shot at a starring role in a feature to return to the United States for a guest shot in a series I'd never heard of? In the vague hope of a blowjob from its star? Or in hopes of landing a recurring second-banana gig? No. Forget it.

Finally, there was a message from someone named Clive.

"Dear sir," he began, "Permit me to introduce myself. I am the head of the Paris chapter of the British Ventura County Appreciation Society. We gather together Saturday evenings for a regular two-and-a-half-hour session of that week's V.C. episodes in English. When I heard that you were here in Paris on an extended stay, I was needless to say thrilled. I wonder if you would consider attending one of our meetings as a surprise for our members?"

Dear God, it sounded ghastly. I was prepared to respond with a polite refusal, but his next lines caught me off guard and awakened my sympathies:

"It would mean so much to our members, most of whom are quite elderly and, frankly, in many cases daft. It would give my own wife Deirdre (who, though of reasonably sound mind, is wheelchair-bound) something to live for."

I responded in a friendly but noncommittal way, suspecting that in the end I would make the visit, beaming a bit of sunshine into their dreary, elderly ex-pat lives.

MARDI, DIX MAI

GINNY ARRIVED THREE DAYS LATER AND phoned me from her hotel. Would I be a dear and come get her for a night out on the town? Unfortunately I had a dinner scheduled with Esmée and her as-yet-unseen husband. What the hell, I thought, invite her along. There's nothing like a porn star to liven up a dull business dinner. Plus, showing up with a date might serve to divert any suspicions he might have about me and his wife.

When I asked for Ginny at the reception they told me she had already left, and then I saw her standing on the sidewalk in front of the hotel in a fur coat completely unsuited to the balmy evening and smoking a cigarette. She was such a magnificent, statuesque creature I couldn't stop myself watching her for a minute. I was approaching to announce myself when another guest of the hotel, an American by the sound of her, stepped up to her.

"Excuse me," the woman said. "Do you know how many animals died to make that coat?"

Unfazed, Ginny took a long, languid drag off of the cigarette. "Do you know how many guys I had to fuck to buy it?" she asked, and as the woman slunk off I laughed out loud.

"Hey, there he is," she said. "Some fucking people, right?"

"Right," I said, as the bell captain whistled for a taxi.

• • •

When we got to the restaurant Esmée and her husband were already seated, and I was glad I hadn't shown up stag. His name was Claude and he didn't appear happy to be there. It looked to me as if he had one hand on Esmée's knee under the table, and not in an affectionate or erotic way; more like he wanted to make sure nobody else's hand touched her there.

Claude asked how I was enjoying the use of their apartment. "I like the neighborhood and it affords a little more privacy than the hotel did."

"What's the idea behind this film of yours?"

I explained the premise briefly, and he asked whether it was a comedy. "It has comedic elements," I told him, and when I expanded on the idea of the megalomaniac art collector he seemed unamused.

"Where did you get that idea?"

"It was your wife's," I said, and he arched an eyebrow and let out a laugh.

"What's her role?"

She was the love interest, obviously. Why else cast a woman of her great beauty? But I had a sense that was the wrong answer, so I came up with something else. "She's the hero's antagonist. A rival archaeologist."

He snorted. "Is that right? Seems like if I'm putting up a good chunk of the budget in order for her to star, she ought to be the female lead. What's the matter, this archaeologist doesn't like girls?"

"Well, see, they start out as bitter rivals and end up in love."

He nodded. "That sounds more like it." He nodded at Ginny. "Where'd you find her?"

"She used to be on the show."

"What show?" he asked. They really hadn't filled him in on any of this.

"It's called *Ventura County*, sort of a soap opera. It's on every night at seven."

"And you wrote this show?"

"No, I was the star."

He was taken aback. "Thought you were writing this thing."

"I'm co-writing it with Frédéric LaForge."

"Am I supposed to know this character?"

"Not necessarily."

"Here's another thing. I want a job for my son on this picture."

"I'm sure that can be arranged." I hoped Bruno had gotten over his desire to do me harm, but I wasn't terrifically worried about it.

"He's a bright kid, but he hasn't found his direction in life. And he can't get over wanting to fuck his stepmother here." He slapped Esmée's thigh and she jumped a little, engaged as she was in a quiet conversation with Ginny, probably trading vaginal-tightening tips or favorite brands of edible spermicidal creams.

• • •

Ginny and I decided to walk back to her hotel after dinner. We were crossing the Pont de l'Alma when a man stepped up to us with his hands behind his back. For a second I tensed, thinking we were about to be mugged, but what he whipped around and pointed in our direction was a camera. The flash went off, and he checked the image on the finder.

"Beautiful," he said, and turned to hurry away.

"Which paper?" I yelled after him, and he turned back to me, still moving away from us at a fast clip.

"All of them," he said, and then disappeared into the crowd.

• • •

It was nearly three in the morning when I got back to my building. Outside the building a sextet of young drunks were gathered outside the nightclub next door, laughing and yelling and shoving one another in what must have been an attempt to grab the attention of the female company they'd failed to attract inside the club. One of them recognized me and shouted, "Hey, Doc!"

I keyed in the code and pushed the door open into the lobby, and before it shut another tenant followed me inside. Late twenties, clothing expensive but self-consciously casual, hair carefully cut into an intentionally disheveled mess, a nasty smirk on his unshaven lip. He was swaying back and forth, propping himself against the wall with one hand and giggling. He was no tenant; the son of a bitch was one of the drunks from the disco next door.

"*Salut*," he slurred.

I ignored him. It was bad form, having let in a stranger and a drunken one at that, but I didn't really care. No one had seen me do it.

"Hey," he said. "I know you, don't I?"

I ignored him.

"Hey," he said, a little louder. "I'm talking to you."

I continued to pretend he wasn't there, though the desire to chuck him out the front door was mounting.

"I'm scaring you, aren't I?" he said with a snicker.

Here's something about being in the public eye: Sometimes you have to be a badass, or else word gets around that you can be manipulated. I liked this neighborhood and I didn't want to have to be looking over my shoulder worrying about the denizens of the club.

So I grabbed the glib bastard by the back of his collar and smashed his face against the marble wall of the foyer. There was a hollow, wooden *thunk*, but that wasn't the sound I was looking for. I took hold of his ears and pushed him forward again and was rewarded with the satisfying crack of a breaking nose. Then I took hold of his collar again with my right hand and stuck two fingers through the belt loop at the back of his pants, frog-marched him to the front door, opened it, and kicked him square in the ass. He went face-first down the steps to the sidewalk, and as he lay there I had to resist the temptation to give him a swift kick to the belly. He rose with some difficulty and moaned as his comrades from the club watched, no longer laughing. I stared one of them down until he looked away; two of them went back inside the club while another walked away, and two of them resumed their conversation, much more quietly.

Finally the drunk got up and looked around. Nose and upper lip bloody, he stumbled away into the night, and I went upstairs to get some sleep.

• • •

Dealing with the drunk had got my adrenaline flowing to a degree it wouldn't have back in the day, though, and sleep wasn't coming, so I put in a DVD of *Full Metal Jacket* and watched the first half of it, the bootcamp section. I've read criticism of the film suggesting that Kubrick intended the bootcamp scenes to underscore the dehumanization necessary for young men to go to war and kill, but I disagree; in embracing the sort of structured violence that allows one to prepare for the unstructured kind—for example, my earlier encounter with the drunk—we become closer to our atavistic selves, connecting our civilized to our pre-civilized natures. At least that's how it was for me. The military turned me from an unformed, unmotivated punk with no discipline and no future into a man, capable of devoting his life to the study of art and the contemplation of beauty and truth and at the same time obligated to take no shit from anyone or anything.

Around the time Private Pyle kills R. Lee Ermey and then himself, I felt sleep closing in, and I switched the set off and bagged it for the night.

MERCREDI, ONZE MAI

GINNY AND I BOTH GOT A LAUGH OUT OF THE article that accompanied the photo from the Pont de l'Alma the next day, which I translated aloud for her:

DR. CRANDALL TAYLOR AMOUREUX D'UNE STAR DE PORNO.

You can't buy that kind of publicity. In fact, sometimes you have to pay people to avoid it. Love, hell; we liked each other well enough, certainly found one another more than reasonably attractive, but there was no more love in it than there was between a couple of ex–race horses being mated in honor of their respective track times. I was temporarily enthralled because she was a porn star, and she was happy to be fucking a television star. She made kind of a game of it, in fact; among my predecessors in her bed had been the bassist for a hair metal band, at least one billionaire CEO, any number of politicians, even a former president of the United States (and don't be too quick to think you can guess which one; the answer would surprise you).

• • •

I got a call from Annick in the afternoon. I hadn't heard from her in days, hadn't, in fact, gotten around to breaking up with her, and she was a little petulant.

"Been keeping yourself busy?" she said.

"Reasonably."

"I hear you and Bruno's dad are fast friends."

Really? "Sure we are."

"How do you like Esmée? I hear she wants to be a star."

"I think she's got it in her."

"So when I ask if I've got it in me to be a star you say, 'Go to acting school,' and when she says it you cast her in your movie."

"You're not married to someone who can finance the picture."

"I want a part in it."

Jesus. This was getting a little complicated. "Sure."

"You're patronizing me," she said. "I don't like that."

She was making me nervous again. I pictured her slitting my throat in my sleep. "No, I'm serious. I'll have Fred come up with a part. A small one, this time. A stepping stone."

"All right," she said, not entirely satisfied.

"Listen, Annick, I've been meaning to give you a shout. You know, with me being in business with Bruno's dad and stepmother, I'm thinking maybe you and I ought to give it a rest for a while."

A long silence on the other end of the line, followed by a deep sigh. "I knew it. You're fucking Esmée, aren't you?"

"Are you crazy?"

"You are. And don't think I don't know about your porn star, either. My mom saw it in the paper."

"That's a fabrication. She's a cast mate, she used to be on the show before she did porn."

"You know what? I don't care. I just want to keep seeing you. Bruno doesn't have to know about it."

Jesus. Unsound as the whole idea was, I wanted to keep fucking her. There was something about her youth and enthusiasm that made me feel young, or at any rate reminded me of what being young had been like.

"All right," I said. "But you can't come to the apartment, there's too much chance Esmée or Bruno will spot you."

"Want to come to my dorm?"

• • •

Annick's dormitory was a late-nineteenth-century building on the Boulevard St. Michel. I checked in at the desk in the cavernous lobby and asked for her. If the lady behind the desk recognized me she gave no sign of it, and while she buzzed for Annick I looked around the lobby. On one wall was an immense oil painting of a portly Edwardian lady in pearls and a diamond tiara, identified on the plaque below as the founder of the institution. A touch on my shoulder made me spin, and I found myself facing Annick.

"You like her?"

"She looks formidable, in the English sense of the word."

"She haunts the place. Come on, you want the grand tour?"

• • •

She took me through a darkened cafeteria on the ground floor. "It's not in use anymore, but the place used to furnish three meals a day for several hundred girls."

"How come you have the keys to the place?" I asked. So far she'd unlocked three massive oaken doors in our progression through the largely disused ground floor.

"I'm an employee as well as a resident. Come on, there's something I want to show you."

She beckoned me, and I followed her down a rickety spiral staircase in the far corner of the cafeteria, behind the service bar. It was pitch black down there, and I had a distinct feeling of dread as we descended.

At the bottom we stood in darkness, and as my eyes grew accustomed to the light I saw that we were in a corner of what was once a large institutional kitchen. We pushed through into the next room, which was dimly illuminated at ceiling level by basement windows. Row after row of ancient cabinets receded into the distance, and I followed her through another door into a long, narrow room.

She flicked a light switch and a fluorescent tube overhead crackled slowly to life. Along the wall were cabinets containing old, unused flatware, and running along the floor on one side were bins; on the other, drawers. One of the bins had broken open to reveal its contents: sawdust.

"What's the sawdust for?" I asked.

"Who knows? It's before my time. Cleaning up vomit, maybe. Look at this, though."

She opened one of the drawers, pulled out a butter knife, and handed it to me. "Check it out."

It was heavy. "Real silver?"

"Tons of it, completely unused. It's a miracle nobody's ever bagged it all up and taken it to the flea market."

There was definitely something not right in the air down there. "I don't suppose this is where the old lady in the painting manifests herself?"

"No, she appears in the music room upstairs, and once in a while when there's music in the cafeteria. Old-fashioned music, I mean; I don't think she's a big hip-hop fan. But I've worked with people who wouldn't come down here by themselves. Supposedly there's an old lady cook who won't leave and doesn't like having people down here."

On the floor was linoleum of a type I'd never seen before, intricately patterned and, near the walls where the wear on it was less severe, still brightly colored.

"What's in there?" I asked her, indicating a large door at the end of the hall with a steel locking mechanism.

"Just what it looks like," she said. "A walk-in meat locker."

I tried the handle, and with a loud, rusty squeal the door came unsealed. From inside came a musty smell of dust, grime, and stale air. Hanging from the ceiling was a single, ancient light bulb with a chain dangling from its socket. I pulled it and heard a click, but it failed to illuminate.

"Seems a shame no one's doing anything with the space," I said.

"Who said no one's doing anything with it?" she said, and went down on one knee, unzipping my fly with a neat stroke as I leaned back against one of the counters in expectation of ecstasy.

Just as she hit her rhythm, though, there was a metallic crash outside the closed door, and her reaction was so startled I counted myself lucky she hadn't bitten my dick off.

She stood and zipped me up, and we slowly opened the door and found that an old brass service tray had fallen from its spot on the wall.

"There's your old lady cook," I said.

"What do you say I sneak you into my room instead?" she said.

• • •

I don't think I'd awakened in a dorm room since I was about twenty. The one into whose windows the setting sun's rays shone was small but comfortable, with a ledge beneath said windows from which Annick sat watching me sleep.

"What time is it?" I asked.

"It's late. You fell asleep right after and I didn't have the heart to wake you."

"I did? That's a new one." And it was; usually I jump out of bed and into the shower and get out of there as quick as I can.

"Guess I sapped your precious bodily fluids."

"There may be something to that." I got up and headed for the sink and, as I didn't care to brave the communal shower Annick had shown me on the way up, washed my dick in it.

Actually, she may have been right about those bodily fluids. To say I've never been the monogamous type would be to understate the matter. In fact, someone once told me I was a textbook case of satyriasis. But even for me it was unusual to be carrying on intensive affairs with four different, sexually demanding women. Maybe, to paraphrase Mick Jagger, I just didn't have that much jam. Tonight, I vowed, oysters.

I decided to take Annick with me, as it seemed ungentlemanly to fuck and run in her case. Marie-Laure or Esmée would have understood, and Ginny would have expected it, but young as she was there were many experiences Annick still lacked, and it would be fun to take her out to the sort of restaurant I had in mind.

We went to a restaurant I used to love when I was a student, over by Les Halles. In those days it was a special treat to eat a half dozen oysters there, washed down with a glass of Alsatian wine, and so now I ordered a mixed dozen oysters apiece along with a bottle of Riesling, and Annick explained to me how she'd ended up with Bruno in the first place.

"We were both writing about John O'Hara. You know him?"

"I know he once beat up a midget in a bar fight."

"That's right. He also once said, 'I have never in my life hit a woman, except in anger.' Anyway, he couldn't get through the reading."

"Bruno couldn't?"

"He has a lot of trouble reading, particularly in English."

"That would seem to be a handicap in a student of American literature."

"I suppose so. Anyway, I ended up reading about half of his course load and describing the plots to him, and then I helped him write the paper."

"That's touching. He needed you."

"It sounds sort of pathetic now, but there was something sweet about him. He did need me, it's true, and I didn't mind."

"Something I don't understand. I thought you told me you lived with Bruno?"

"He has an apartment; I live there about half the time. When I'm working at the foyer, though, I have to sleep there. It's also nice to have a place to retreat to when he's being an asshole. Which is a lot."

We were seated in a banquette by the window, and it was difficult for the other diners to get a glimpse of us. I kind of missed the attention, but at the same time it allowed me to massage her thigh unmolested.

"So what do you know about Claude?" I asked.

"Bruno's dad? He's not around much, for one thing."

"What exactly is his line of work? I don't imagine investing in oddball nightclubs is what made his fortune."

She looked a little uncomfortable. I always forget about that French reluctance to speak about money, even to discuss what one does for a living. In America it's sex we don't discuss. (Most of us don't, anyway; I'd be short of things to say if I followed that particular cultural taboo.) But I pressed her; it was important, since he was theoretically going to be in business with me, and since I was banging his lovely wife.

"I was wondering if it was some sort of import-export business, since he travels so much."

She looked down at the three oysters that remained. One of them was so big it looked like the giant gray tongue of a calf.

"Come on," I said. "I thought you were planning to go to the States someday. You'll have to get used to this kind of vulgar talk."

"It's not that," she said, looking very uncomfortable. I realized for the first time that her eyes were not quite identical. One of them was blue, the other a sort of bluish green. "It's just that it's something Bruno told me in secret."

"You can tell me," I said, massaging that thigh, moving up the leg a bit toward her midsection.

She leaned forward and said in a loud stage whisper, "He sells weapons."

That put a new spin on things. I tried to sound unimpressed. "Is that so? Guns and such?"

"Guns, missiles, artillery. Bruno thinks he might be dealing nukes with North Korea."

No shit. I was fucking the wife of an arms dealer, the kind of guy for whom killing really meant nothing at all. Cool.

• • •

I dropped her off in a taxi on the Boulevard de Sébastopol and started walking toward the Left Bank. The occasional passerby stopped and called out to me, to which I returned a snappy salute, and at Châtelet one old lady stopped me to lecture me about my character's love life.

"That pretty nurse, why do you treat her that way? She should be making you babies! There's more to life than making love to strange women, doctor."

I thanked her, promised to consider it, and was on my way.

• • •

I decided to walk along the river and descended to the Quai du Louvre. As I crossed beneath the Pont du Carousel I heard someone snicker from the shadows, followed by more snickering from several individuals, followed by a suggestion that some cocksucker be killed for his shit. Sensing that I was the cocksucker in question, I reached into my vest pocket and removed the tactical baton.

"Uh, 'scuse me, sir, you dropped something," came a voice from behind me.

I spun and faced a guy in his twenties carrying a blade with no idea how to use it offensively. From beneath the bridge came four of his comrades, at least one of them a girl, judging from the giggling.

"All right, faggot, let's see the wallet. And the watch, and that way you don't get fucked up."

"Goodness gracious me," I said, the joyful adrenaline flowing through my veins and counteracting the pacifying effect of the oysters and wine in my belly. "Want my phone, too?"

"Fuck yeah, I want your fucking phone, bitch, hand it the fuck over."

I flicked the baton under and over and hit his hand, and the knife went flying into the river with a satisfying, plosive splash. Before he'd fully processed its loss I cracked him across his teeth and kicked him hard in the balls, and he went down to the paving stones howling.

His friends hesitated, and then the girl said, "Are you gonna let that faggot kick René's ass like that, bitch?"

At that one of them charged me, a large fellow with a stupid look on his face, at least as far as I could tell in the dim light of the quai. He was open for one of the real textbook moves in judo, so I de-telescoped the baton and, just before impact, replaced it in my jacket pocket. I bent down, stepped slightly aside and altered his trajectory over my shoulder and down the stones of the embankment and then down into the Seine to join his friend's blade.

(I used to hear that if you fell into the Seine they automatically hospitalized you and gave you a serious, heavy-duty course of antibiotics. Is that still true, or was it ever? Or is it just one of those things they tell young American exchange students to discourage them from diving into the river?)

"*Au suivant*," I yelled, and two of them turned and ran. The girl stumbled forward.

"Fucking faggots, afraid of some stupid fucking bitch. Come on, cunt, let's get it on."

She, too, had a knife, and like her friend she was holding it all wrong. The baton didn't seem sporting fighting a girl, so I waited until she was close and starting to lunge, and then I planted my right fist in her belly as hard as I'd ever hit anyone, male or female.

Something about it felt wrong, though, and when she hit the ground I saw that she was pregnant. I took the knife, which had fallen from her hand, and threw it into the river, and then I climbed the steps to the bridge and crossed it. I walked some distance trying to find a pay phone (there's the curse of the cell phone; never a pay phone around when you want to make a call that can't be traced to you later) and finally found one by going the wrong direction, just off the Place St. Michel.

I called the SAMU and informed them that a young woman was lying unconscious beneath the Pont du Carousel and that she seemed to be pregnant, and then I hung up.

On the way home I heard the ambulance's Klaxon honking and wished the girl well despite it all. Mostly I hoped I'd terminated that pregnancy, though inadvertently, if only for the sake of the kid himself. I grew up with a mother like that and buddy, that's not any way you want to grow up.

JEUDI, DOUZE MAI

MY MOM WAS MARRIED FOR THE FIRST TIME at fourteen (illegally) and divorced at seventeen. She had got her GED and started college, an experiment that produced nothing but a second marriage, to the instructor of her freshman math course, which itself was the result of a pregnancy that began in the classic American manner, in the backseat of a Thunderbird. My father, with whom I maintained sporadic contact until his death, was overjoyed at the prospect of a child, but my mother didn't take to it. She found that what she liked was drinking and other fellows and, after the unpleasant surprise of my arrival, birth control. I do have one sister, fifteen years my junior, from my mother's third marriage and brief flirtation with sobriety and Christianity; my stepfather, a good and honest if somewhat stern Kentuckian, suffered through five years of her antics before divorcing her. I'm in somewhat spotty contact with him and my sister, though whether my mother is still among the living is a matter of some indifference to me.

Anyway, my discovery after my discharge that acting was something I was good at and that women liked was probably what saved me from a life of brawling and petty criminality. All that anger gets wrapped up in the preparation and chucked out in the performance. An art therapist once told me that all art is art therapy.

• • •

I was in bed telling all this to Esmée the next night. I'd spent the day wondering about the girl under the bridge and was rewarded in the late afternoon with an account on the *Libération* website about a group of young people who claimed they'd been beaten up by Dr. Crandall Taylor from the television. Two of them had been hospitalized; there was no mention of a third, which either meant that the first boy hadn't been hurt very badly or that the one I'd tossed into the Seine had floated away. There was no mention of the girl's being pregnant, which presumably meant she hadn't miscarried. My feelings were mixed there, but I'm not the Pope and it wasn't my business to go around deciding who could or couldn't reproduce.

Esmée had shown up around seven, and we spent some time looking at the artwork before surrendering to the bedroom's pull. When we were done I asked where the money had come from to buy all that artwork.

"Some of it's mine, from modeling."

"You earned enough modeling to buy a Picasso?"

"Please, it's a little drawing."

"They're not giving those little drawings away. What does Claude do for a living, anyway?"

This was the moment of truth. I didn't care if it was true or not, I just wanted to see if she'd tell me.

"He's in the import-export trade."

"Where is he now?" I was thinking North Korea or Iran, or maybe Pakistan or Israel.

"I don't know. He doesn't tell me where he goes. Anyway, he won't be back for a week."

"Would he kill me if he knew?"

She snorted. "Don't be melodramatic."

"But he doesn't like me, does he?"

"No."

"Is he going to put up the money for the movie?"

She extended a long leg into the air above the bed and studied its perfection. "I hate to say this, but I don't think he is."

"You say you've got money from modeling. Enough to buy a little Picasso drawing."

"All right, he paid for that. But I picked it out."

"Isn't it your money, too? Can't you insist?"

"It's not that kind of marriage. I'm still working on him. Don't despair."

"I'm not desperate yet. Tomorrow I'm going to go out to Longchamp and bet all I've got left in the world on a horse in the fifth."

She took in a deep breath and sat up, once again with that charming gesture of placing her hand flat on her sternum, taking my little joke quite seriously. "You mustn't."

"Why not?"

"Tomorrow's Friday the thirteenth."

I laughed and thought to myself maybe I would go to the track tomorrow for real. Esmée left before midnight with a stern warning not to do anything the next day that required any sort of luck, and I went to sleep earlier than usual, convinced that my own luck was almost magically good and that no harm would come to me, little suspecting that downstairs was a man with a gun and a key to the apartment and a seething desire to see me dead.

VENDREDI, TREIZE MAI

AND SO WE ARRIVE BACK AT THE POINT where I had Claude Guiteau—arms dealer, jealous husband, would-be assassin—tied unconscious to a chair in an apartment he and his wife owned.

Rather pleased with myself just by virtue of being alive, I went down to the basement storage area where Esmée kept her spare luggage and opened the padlock. I seemed to remember a large, old steamer trunk plastered with labels from all over the world like you see in old movies. Sure enough, there it was, and it seemed to me that the stickers with their retro graphics might have some value. Whoever had owned the trunk back in the day had been around: Marrakesh, Buenos Aires, Kyoto, San Francisco. It was a big one, too, though I wasn't sure it would be big enough. I'd seen a movie once where a man was stuffed inside one of these prior to being killed, and I remembered being unconvinced that a big man would really fit inside one.

Upstairs Fred was scribbling on a sheet of paper, seemingly oblivious to the slobbering, comatose figure seated across the kitchen from him. I left the trunk by the door and stood over his shoulder. He looked up at me, annoyed. "Let me think," he said.

"Whatever you're writing down, you'd better be prepared to chew up and swallow," I told him.

"Don't worry, it's all in code."

"Chew it up and swallow it," I said. "Prosecuting attorneys love shit like that. I should know, I've played a few."

He dropped the pen. "Look, I don't know what to tell you right now. I think we're both in a lot of trouble. You, especially."

"What if I just call the cops and say he came into my apartment and tried to shoot me? I could untie him and take the gag out and nobody'd be the wiser."

"I don't know. It's his apartment, after all."

"Doesn't matter. I'm in possession of it at the moment, that makes it my domicile and I have a right to defend myself therein. It's a well-established point of jurisprudence."

He opened his mouth but didn't speak, and his eyes rolled upward in exasperation at my obtuseness. Fred had no poker face. "American jurisprudence."

"You mean the principle doesn't apply here?"

"How should I know? I'm no lawyer. All I'm saying is you should tread very carefully. Anyway, it doesn't look like you're planning to call the cops." He nodded in the direction of the trunk. "Looks more like you're planning to get rid of a body."

"Not a body. I can't keep him here, though. What if he wakes up? What if the neighbors hear him kicking? And Esmée is sure to be back for one thing or another."

"Which is what got us into this situation in the first place. Okay, where are we going to take him?"

"I've got a place, and if we're lucky we can do it tonight."

I dialed Annick's cell phone, and when she answered she sounded wide awake. "It's me. Where are you?"

"I've got the overnight shift at the front desk," she said, and I felt the hair on my arms prickle as though an electrical storm were about to break out. My good fortune was holding out.

"Can I ask you for a big favor?" I asked.

"How big?" she asked, her voice slow with suspicion.

• • •

Fred went down to the taxi stand at Odéon and brought one back to the front of the building where I stood guarding the trunk (though I have to admit that it would have been pretty fucking funny if someone had stolen it). The cab was a station wagon, and the driver and I lifted our burden into the back of it with a single coordinated heave. I was wearing dark glasses and a baseball cap, and I didn't think he knew me, but I made a point of letting Fred do all the talking, and when we got to the address on the Boulevard St. Michel, Fred handed the driver the fare plus a fifteen percent tip—not so cheap he'd resent it, and not so generous we'd stand out from his usual late-night clientele.

I spotted a sewer grate on the sidewalk, and I took Claude's pistol from my pocket and tossed it in, noting with satisfaction the splash and clatter of metal against concrete. With the next big rain it would be swept down to the Seine. I remember being quite proud at that moment of having had the presence of mind to get rid of the thing.

I rapped on the door, and after opening the judas to verify my identity Annick let us in.

"What's in that?" she asked.

"It might be better if you didn't know. Just something I need to store in that meat locker downstairs for a few days."

She stood with her arms folded across that lovely young chest. "If you don't tell me what it is, you can fuck off."

Fred looked at me in a panic. What the hell, I thought, she's right. This is her job, and she could lose it if she were to help me in storing heroin or weapons. I leveled with her.

"It's the arms dealer."

She frowned, not quite understanding. "I'm sorry? You don't mean Bruno's dad?"

I nodded and pointed to the trunk. "He tried to kill me. Can we put him in the meat locker while I figure out what to do with him?"

"A corpse? You want me to conceal a corpse? You've got to be fucking kidding me."

"He's alive."

She thought about it. "He really tried to kill you?"

"Came to the apartment with a gun, fired it into what he thought was my head." I made a pistol out of my fingers and fired: *blam*. "You told me nobody goes down there."

She let out a sigh. "Twenty-four hours. No more. And if you end up killing him you can't do it here."

"No problem."

"And I want a part in your movie."

Ah, there it was. She had no more business acting than I had performing thoracic surgery, but what could I say?

"Done," I said.

• • •

If the place was spooky in the daytime, it was a regular chamber of horrors at night. Since Annick was on desk duty, we were on our own once she showed us the way down via the freight elevator and turned on the lights. As soon as we got him into the locker I opened up the trunk and found him still breathing, which in and of itself was a cause for celebration, since it hadn't occurred to Fred or me that we might want to ventilate the lid for him. I grabbed an old cafeteria chair from the kitchen and brought it into the locker, then I stole a scalding-hot light bulb from an overhead socket, tossing it from hand to hand as I took it back to the dangling socket in the locker.

When I was done there was a light on overhead and Claude was securely tied to that chair with the bright blue ball gag in his mouth.

"What happens when he wakes up?" Fred said.

"Nothing happens," I said. "He's in a fucking meat locker."

"I mean what if he starts yelling?"

"That's what the gag's for."

"I don't know how effective that'll be."

"Go inside, I'll close the door and you yell."

He hesitated, but he went inside and I locked the door. From within came Fred's scream, one that would have done an actor proud, so horrific that I wondered for a moment whether Claude had escaped his bonds and attacked him. But I could only just hear it through the steel door, and there was no way anyone upstairs would. I opened the door and told him it was all right.

"What now?" Fred asked.

"I don't know about you," I said, "but I could use some shut-eye."

• • •

I awoke at noon to the ringing of my cell phone. It was Marie-Laure wanting to know if I could escort her to a cocktail party, among whose guests was a director she wanted me to meet. "Absolutely," I said, and having written down the coordinates I hung up the phone and realized I was starving. I dressed and went downstairs and around the corner to the café, stopping to pick up the newspapers on the way. Settled in at my usual table on the sidewalk, I ordered an *omelette mixte* and a double espresso and started in on the devilishly tricky Saturday crossword in the *Herald Tribune*.

The omelette was perfect, and I inhaled it like a starving man. The day was cool and most of the passersby looked a degree or two happier than I would have expected. Perhaps I was projecting onto them my own feelings of well-being, my sense that I was finally in the right place at the right time. Once I'd finished the eggs I lingered over the cooling coffee, and when I was done I ordered another.

Once again I found myself with one unanswerable clue in the middle of the puzzle. As I pondered the empty spaces my phone went off again, chiming Fred's ringtone. I almost didn't answer, then decided to ask him for help with the puzzle. "Fred," I said, "what's a twelve-letter word meaning 'surgical removal of a patch of skull'? It's a variant spelling. In English, please."

He was silent for a moment, then in a burst of enthusiasm spoke up. "Trephination. Variant of trepanation."

I tried it out, and with that one filled in, half a dozen other answers suddenly presented themselves. "Excellent."

"So, have you been yet?"

"Been where?"

Again, silence on the other end of the line. Then, a hesitant tone, as though gauging my seriousness: "To the place we were at before?"

"Which place?" I was still halfway working on the puzzle and in no mood for guessing games.

"The place we left our friend last night?"

And then I remembered. Absolutely amazing, the power of the human mind to sweep unpleasantness aside when the body or the mind is in need of repose. Until that moment I hadn't given a nanosecond's thought to last night's adventure. To be suddenly reminded of it, and of the delicate situation he and I were in, along with Annick, should have sickened me, but it had the opposite effect; I felt as though we were involved in a jolly adventure.

"Ah. No, I haven't been. Perhaps we should go."

"We?"

"Well, when he comes to he's likely to assume he's being held by some extremist group. If he sees me, he'll know that's not the case. And Annick is his son's girlfriend. You, on the other hand, are unknown to him. Do you see the logic?"

"I suppose I do."

"We'll have to arrange it with Annick. Maybe she can let you in some other way than the front door. Take him a sandwich or something, and let me know what happens. And hey, why don't you take your laptop and work on the script while you're down there? Maybe you'll get inspired."

• • •

The party was held at the home of a famous record producer. At least I was told he was famous, the name didn't mean anything to me. Marie-Laure led me through the crowd as though on a leash, introducing me to various movers and shakers and finally to Roberto Casselini, the director she wanted me to meet.

"Very pleased to meet you," he said with an Italian accent as heavy as my American one. "I watch your program regularly."

"We've been talking about your project, and Roberto is very interested," Marie-Laure said.

"Yes, of course, the Venus de Milo, she's Italian—maybe we can get some funding from Rome as well."

Pointing out to him that the Venus was actually a representation of Aphrodite, and of Greek origin to boot, would have been counterproductive, so I kept quiet. "What sorts of things have you directed?" I asked.

"Lots of TV movies, a couple of low-budget features back home in Italy. I think this could go theatrical. How far along is the script?"

"It'll be ready soon," I said, the thought hitting me that the more time Fred had to waste playing nursemaid to Claude, the less time he had to write our script. I was going to have to reexamine our priorities.

"And I understand you have the lovely Mlle. DeHoving as leading lady."

"Who?" I asked.

"Esmée," Marie-Laure said. "That's her professional name."

"Ah. Yes." For obvious reasons I actually preferred to think of her as Mlle. DeHoving rather than as Mme. Guiteau, especially at present.

"And what's her role, precisely?" Roberto asked.

"Sort of a femme fatale," I said, and as I said it I was suddenly aware of how meaningless that phrase was.

Because really, aren't they all?

SAMEDI, QUATORZE MAI

I REALLY SHOULD HAVE HEADED DOWN TO THE dormitory and relieved poor Frédéric, but Marie-Laure had mentioned before our arrival that her husband was out of town, casually adding how exciting she always found extramarital sex in the marital bed. It excited me, too, to be honest, and so around 2:00 AM we got into the company car and the driver, whose name I had finally learned was Balthazar, took us to her apartment in Neuilly.

"I'm right by the American Hospital, in case you hurt yourself," she said, and I told her the story of how I'd once gone to its emergency room as a young student with a case of food poisoning. "It was the fifteenth of August, my regular doctor was out of town, and his summer replacement wouldn't see me on a holiday. Violently ill as I was, I wanted something familiar and comforting, so I took a taxi to the American Hospital.

"There was a British doctor on call—he might have been a Scot. He told me I'd eaten something bad and told me to fast until I had a solid bowel movement."

"Did you?"

"I didn't eat for four days. I was starving, so naturally I wasn't shitting at all, solid or otherwise. So I went back. Irish doctor this time. He asks what's the matter, I tell him. He says no, you can't eat until you've had a solid stool. 'But I'm hungry,' I tell him. 'What do you want me to do, cook you a meal?' he says, the glib son of a bitch. So I go back to my tiny studio and I don't eat for another week. Finally I thought, fuck it, I'm eating, and I started eating some white rice, and within a day or two I was fine. When my regular doctor got back and heard about it he was furious, said they never should have told me to fast at all, certainly not for ten days. Told me never to go to the American Hospital again under any circumstances."

We stopped in front of one of those massive stone buildings from the turn of the twentieth century. An apartment in there must cost a fortune, I thought, and, vulgar, money-obsessed American that I am, I wondered whether Marie-Laure's husband earned as much as she did.

"Good night, Balthazar," she said as we got out of the car and the driver pulled away. She pressed her code into the keypad on the door and I pushed the door open. The elevator was tiny, and once inside with the doors closed, we made out like teenagers. I was as aroused and happy as though it were our first time, and sticking my hand inside her skirt and past the elastic of her panties, I started massaging her.

I pushed the ARRÉT button and we hung there, suspended, clawing at one another. "Let's do it right here," I whispered into her ear.

Her voice was throaty and hoarse. "Oh, God," she said, trembling. "I'd love that, but I make too much noise."

She started the cage moving again, straightening herself up as our upward progress resumed, and by the time the door opened with a metallic clunk she looked like any other *haute bourgeoise* in Neuilly sharing an aloof, awkward, silent elevator ride with a stranger.

Once inside the apartment she was a savage again, breathing obscenities. I shoved her onto a couch in the living room, lifted her skirt, and started pulling my cock out.

"Not here," she said. "On the bed."

Fine with me. I slung her over my shoulder, carried her into the bedroom, and tossed her onto the bed.

"Caveman," she said. "Primitive." She pressed her face down to the bedcover and lifted her ass into the air, pulling down her panties to her knees. "Go ahead. I won't fight."

• • •

Half an hour later we lay under her covers and I was wondering to myself why exactly I'd felt so compelled to fuck Esmée, knowing the trouble it might cause, when I had this stunning and imaginatively randy creature at my disposal. She was going on at some length about a way to structure the deal with another TV network, a film studio, and a private investor, and I wasn't paying very close attention until she mentioned Claude.

"Of course he'd be the key to the whole thing, since he'll be putting up first. What's your take on him? Is he in?"

"I think he is," I said. "I think above all he wants Esmée happy, and that's what it's going to take."

"I should tell you I've heard some pretty unsavory stories about him."

"Is that right?"

"You know how he makes his living?"

"Import-export, something in that line."

She snorted. "Something. He's an arms dealer, one of the big ones. He started out brokering American weaponry and branched out. Now he sells to anybody who can pay, and according to a friend in the Ministry of Defense, the government thinks he deals in smuggled fissionable materials as well as finished nukes."

"Wow," I said, feigning surprise.

"So how do you feel about that? About taking that kind of money?"

The truth—that I just wanted to get my movie made—wasn't a very satisfactory answer, so I came up with something a bit more uplifting. "I guess one way to look at it is we're leading him toward a better way."

She was silent for a moment, and then she started giggling. I wasn't quite sure how to take it, so I chuckled, which sent her into further paroxysms of laughter. It took her two or three minutes to catch her breath enough to speak.

"My God," she said. "I'm really going to watch myself. I could just about fall in love with you, you know that?"

The thought fascinated and terrified me, because I realized as she said it that the reverse was true. If there was an ideal woman in the world for me, it was her. I took advantage of the lull in conversation to dress, then I kissed her goodnight and called a taxi.

• • •

I had the cab drop me off at Odéon, and as I walked I phoned Fred, who was not at all happy to speak to me. "I had to get him a bucket," he said.

"A bucket? What for?"

"For a fucking toilet. I can't exactly let him take the elevator upstairs to the shitter, can I?"

"I guess not."

"And guess who has the privilege of wiping the prisoner's ass and dumping the bucket in the toilet?"

"Listen, I promise we'll get this dealt with in a day or two. You get any work done on the script?"

He was quiet for a second, and I braced for an explosion. "I got about fifteen pages."

"That's great. What's the total now?"

"Twenty-five."

"There you go! Can't wait to read 'em."

"Are you coming tomorrow?"

"Sure. I don't suppose you've made any progress in putting together a plan of action."

"For Guiteau? No."

Typical writer, head in the clouds, bitching and moaning about having to wipe someone's ass but not putting any thought into how to get out of the situation. "All right," I said. "I'll come up with something. I promise, no more than a day or two more of toilet duty."

• • •

I got up ten-ish and went downstairs for a walk. It was time to give some serious thought to making my stay here permanent. If the film went over well, I might have a real starring career here. Look at Terence Fisher and Bud Spencer. Look at Eddie Constantine. All right, so they weren't really Americans, but from the start they were sold as Americans, and that was the image they projected, even when the audience knew they weren't. I could fill that niche now.

I got to Les Halles without being importuned by any fans, for which I was grateful. I was also grateful, though, for the fact that people were making friendly eye contact and jostling one another to point out my presence among them. I stopped in at a café with a view of the Fontaine des Innocents, and as I drank my coffee I tried to imagine the place a couple of hundred years ago when it was still part of the old cemetery but already part of the food market, with prostitutes plying their trade amidst the open burial pits. What an amazing combination of basic human needs to be met in one insalubrious locale, and what a city this must have been in those days. I think I would have loved it even more back then.

DIMANCHE, QUINZE MAI

WHEN THE DAWN BROKE ON SUNDAY I WAS seated at the massive oak desk in the apartment, trying to think my way out of the mess I'd created. I'd awakened at five-thirty, suddenly and gravely troubled by the whole business of Claude and the question of what to do with him, and at seven on the dot my cell rang. It was Esmée.

"I think I may be in some trouble," she said. "I had a call from one of Claude's business associates, and he's not where he's supposed to be."

"Where's that?"

"I don't know," she said. "They won't tell me that. But they did tell me they thought he was in Paris a few days ago, just an overnighter. If he was, he didn't let me know he was here. I'm worried."

"What do you suppose happened?"

"I don't know. But we'd better cool it for a while. I have a funny feeling he may have dropped out of sight just to track us and catch us at something."

"Understood." On the one hand, I was frustrated at the thought of avoiding Esmée for what I knew was an unnecessary fear. On the other, though, this left me with only three women to juggle instead of four, and with all I had on my plate at the moment that was probably an advantage. "Call me if there are any developments."

• • •

I went down to the café and sat on the terrace drinking my usual double espresso and considering my options. This time when my cell rang it was Annick. I almost didn't answer—it couldn't really be good news, after all—but she'd gamely allowed me to put her into a difficult and possibly dangerous situation, and I owed her a response. Besides, I might want to pay her a visit later in the day.

"How much longer is he going to be here?" she asked as soon as I said hello.

"And a sunny good morning to you, miss."

"I'm not kidding. Your writer friend is creeping me out, and I'm scared we're going to get found out."

"Everything's going to be fine, just give it a day or two more to play itself out."

"Play itself out? Jesus, you really didn't come into this with any kind of plan at all, did you? Just kidnap one of the richest and most dangerous men in Europe and dump him in a meat locker . . ."

"Whoa, hold on there, missy. There was no kidnapping involved. He broke in and tried to kill me. I knocked him out and had to stash him someplace until I figured out what to do."

"That's an admirably nuanced appraisal. I still need you to make something happen, pronto."

"Understood. Listen, I was thinking I might come over this afternoon."

"Good. Your friend could use some relief."

"I don't mean that, I mean I'd like to see you, is all."

She laughed. "You've got to be shitting me. You're not laying a hand on me until this whole business is dealt with, understand?"

Then she hung up on me. I was a little miffed at the whole situation, particularly the suggestion that I'd kidnapped Claude, as though I were doing it for personal gain and not self-preservation.

And then I began to consider the possibilities. How many groups around the world—right-wing, left-wing, fundamentalist, nationalist—had grudges against Claude Guiteau? How credible would it seem if one of these groups made some demands in the press?

• • •

I went to a news kiosk on the Champs-Élysée and picked up my usual assortment of papers, plus one in Arabic and one in Hebrew. Just to keep things politically murky, I also picked up *l'Humanité* and *Présent*.

Then I stopped into Monoprix and bought a couple of balaclavas from a very pretty blond shopgirl who looked like she was going to wet her pants at the sight of me. "I'm thinking about taking a little ski trip," I said. She was really quite an attractive girl, it seemed to me, and I got her cell number, thinking that when this was all over and done with I might actually go on such a trip, and I might take this excitable young thing with me.

Next I stopped into the FNAC and bought an inexpensive digital pocket camera, one I wouldn't feel bad about throwing away if it became necessary once the photos I needed had been taken and uploaded. I signed an autograph for the mother of the clerk who sold it to me, and, using his own camera phone, one of his colleagues snapped a picture of us arm in arm, like the greatest of pals.

• • •

In the taxi I worked on the *Herald Tribune*'s crossword and found myself stymied by several clues in the middle of the grid, though just as we arrived at the entry to the Luxembourg Gardens (couldn't have a record of me being dropped off too near the building), I scored what I thought was a coup: "ramphorhyncus," for "Winged Jurassic piscivore." I crossed the boulevard a good distance from the dorm and skulked along the back streets with my dark glasses and cap on, still going over that damned crossword in my head.

Where the tiny rue de l'Abbé de l'Épée meets the rue St. Jacques is the old Institution des Sourds-Muets, where the celebrated doctor Jean Itard treated and educated Victor, the wild child of the Aveyron, in the earliest part of the nineteenth century; Truffaut made a movie of it in the sixties. This I learned from a plaque affixed to its wall, directly across from which was a narrow alleyway that led to a rear door to the dormitory, which Annick opened at my signal.

She led me down to the labyrinthine basement and to the meat locker, outside of which sat Fred, typing frantically on his laptop. He looked up at me, surprised, and grinned. "I've come up with some great stuff. It's amazing how much good it does, a little change of scenery."

He went on about some plot twists he had in mind while I nodded intently, one eye still on the crossword. "That all sounds good to me," I said.

"Thanks."

"Hey, have you got anything for 'Fassbinder's '89 nemesis'? Twelve letters, starts with a *k*."

He looked away. "You weren't even listening. You were doing that fucking crossword puzzle in your head."

"I was multitasking. You have a nefarious art thief tangled up with a beautiful woman he enlists to seduce our hero to get the arms, and in the course of the picture she changes sides."

He let out a sigh, not completely satisfied but not angry anymore either. "Krysmopompas."

I thought he was cursing me. "Should I be insulted?"

"It's your answer. Fassbinder's '89 nemesis was a shadowy group called Krysmopompas. It's a movie."

"Wasn't Fassbinder already dead by '89?"

"It was made in '82, the title was *Kamikaze 1989.*"

I had him spell it for me. It fit perfectly, and the rest of the puzzle was the work of forty-five seconds.

"Glad to be of service," he said. "Can we get down to business now?"

• • •

I explained the plan to him and to Annick. "Shouldn't we be holding guns?" she said. "In the picture?"

"You're right," I said, "we should, but I don't know where to get one, and anyone could spot a fake one. How about some knives?"

"You know, I think there's a drawerful somewhere of butcher knives. Let me go look."

She returned in less than five minutes with a pair of lethal-looking blades, though on closer examination they were dull as a child's safety scissors, having gone unsharpened for more than half a century.

Annick and I put our balaclavas on, hers with her long ponytail sticking out of it and hanging down her back, and I opened the meat locker. There sat Claude, still bound to that rotting old chair, the ball gag hanging beneath his chin, unfastened. There was a stench in the room as a reminder of what poor Fred had had to endure over the past couple of days as combination jailer and toilet attendant, and I was surprised to note an air of defiance in Claude's eyes.

"What now?" he asked, and I almost told him to shut up, but I kept my mouth shut. Logic should have told him that I was the one holding him, but I didn't know how much the blows to his head had damaged his brain, and let's face it, when you're an arms merchant on his scale and you've been unconscious for a few hours you really can't tell who's taken custody of you in the interim.

I reached down for the ball gag and reinserted it into his mouth, forcing it way back before cinching it tight. The insolence on his face got a little more pronounced; he might be helpless, but he would not be humiliated. His look of weary contempt reminded me of that old photo of Aldo Moro in the hands of the Red Brigades.

And then inspiration struck. I asked Annick to go get a thick black marker, and when she returned with one I laid the newspapers out across the floor and wrote in large letters: **KRYSMOPOMPAS**.

Annick and I stood behind Claude holding the newspapers while Fred took the pictures with my brand-new camera. When we were done we locked him back in and I thanked Fred for the good work.

"Now which one of you wants to go to an Internet rental place, set up one of those anonymous e-mail accounts, and send these pics to the newspapers? I'd say of the two of you Fred's the less memorable. No offense, Fred, it's purely a question of tits and ass."

• • •

I stopped for lunch at a café across from the Cluny and thought about taking a tour, but my heart wasn't in tourism at the moment. I had a film to produce, and I had just begun to consider that Esmée might not be able to free up Claude's money in his absence. A lot of people were depending on me to pull this deal off, and I was determined not to let them down.

I had finished my *pavé de rumsteak* when my phone rang. Normally I don't take phone calls at table, but when you're dining alone who's to say what the rules are? It was my agent, exasperated.

"Your audition's tomorrow. Where are you?"

"And a big sunny hello to you, too, Bunny, old chum."

"Cut the shit. Where are you?"

"Across from the Cluny, finishing up a nice big lunch. You ought to come over and join me."

"This is it. You get on that plane and be there for that audition tomorrow or we're through. Understand?"

"You'll be singing a different tune when I get this picture made, Bunny."

"Tomorrow, Sunset Gower Studios, Second Front Productions. 3:00 PM."

The son of a bitch hung up on me. I contemplated phoning him back when I saw that I had a text message. It was from Clive, of the Paris chapter of the British *Ventura County* Appreciation Society:

"Wondering if this evening would be a good one to make a surprise visit—having a meeting with several of our Scots members present, and my Deirdre has just learned she's losing a foot, so an appearance from you would be a most timely treat."

What had seemed like a ghastly prospect a few nights ago now sounded like a welcome diversion. I texted him back asking for directions, and once he'd responded I paid my bill, crossed the street, and took that Cluny tour after all.

• • •

Clive and his wife lived in an ill-tended building in the tenth arrondissement not far from where Fred lived. I crossed the courtyard to staircase B and climbed up to the fifth floor, whose carpet was worn to the nub. I could hear a television blaring a football game from one of the apartments and what sounded like an elderly woman sobbing disconsolately in another. I wondered for a moment if it might be poor afflicted Deirdre, but the apartment number was wrong.

At the end of the hallway was a door with paint flaking off it and a yellow note stuck to it next to the peephole. In English it read VENTURA COUNTY APPRECIATION SOCIETY MEETING, COME ON IN.

I knocked, and from inside came a shrill, scratchy, British-accented lady's voice, again in English: "Come on in, dear." There was a Monty Python–esque quality to the sound of it, that of a man imitating a woman and rather badly, but I put that down to Deirdre's dire medical state and pushed the door open anyway.

The apartment appeared empty at first glance, the entryway dark and unencumbered by coats or shoes or even a doormat, and I walked through to the parlor to find it just as empty, a thin, diffused light coming in through moth-eaten curtains onto a bare and badly decaying carpet.

"Just a moment, dearie," came that voice from what I assumed was the kitchen, and I crossed the parlor calling for Clive.

When I pushed the door open to the kitchen I took a bad blow to the temple that had me on my knees. A male voice, an American one, whispered in my ear from behind:

"Next time I'll kill you, you son of a bitch," he said, and then came another blow, this one to the base of my skull.

• • •

It was dark when I regained consciousness and pulled myself up to my feet. I still had my cell phone and called for an ambulance, and while I waited for it to arrive downstairs I took stock of the place. It was empty and looked to have been so for quite some time. The lock on the front door had been broken, and the note about the fictional Paris chapter of the British *Ventura County* Appreciation Society was gone.

They took me to the Hôpital Fernand-Widal, where a series of jovial doctors and nurses, having quickly come to the as-yet-unsubstantiated opinion that nothing was seriously wrong with me, paraded before me, joking about having a famous doctor in their midst and asking me my opinion regarding various minor ailments of their own, to which I responded with a good cheer I did not honestly feel (the one exception being a rather attractive fiftyish nurse who, certain we were alone for a moment, flashed me her quite extraordinary tits, asked if I thought they looked normal, and, winking, passed me her phone number).

At length the results of my MRI came in, and a grim neurologist explained to me that, despite his grim demeanor, I had sustained no concussion or serious injury and as soon as I'd spoken to the police I could leave.

"The police?"

"You were assaulted, monsieur. They'll want to file a report." He chuckled. "And they'll want to be able to tell their wives they met you in the line of duty."

I certainly didn't mind. Someone had gone to some trouble to set a trap for me, and I wanted to find him. "When do they get here?" I asked.

"They're waiting outside right now." He tapped his clipboard on my knee and told me to get dressed, and as soon as I'd cinched my belt the door opened. There were two of them, both exuding businesslike indifference to the situation and my standing as a celebrity. If I didn't know better I'd have almost said they didn't recognize me, but the taller and younger of the two kept looking me up and down appraisingly, a common enough reaction to seeing a two-dimensional acquaintance in three dimensions for the first time.

The older one cleared his throat and introduced himself as Inspector Bonnot. "The doctor says you sustained no serious damage. That was lucky. Getting knocked unconscious in real life is a lot more dangerous than it is on the television."

"Tell me about it," I said. "I've been hit on the head so many times on the TV my character should be a drooling vegetable by now."

"Tell us how it happened."

I started with the first text message, which I'd saved. At his request I forwarded both messages to his mobile, and he read both quietly while his partner murmured how much his wife enjoyed *Ventura County*.

"This *Ventura County* Appreciation Society—is this something you've heard of before?"

"Not that I know of. There are a few fan clubs here and there, though."

"Have you received any sort of threat recently? Credible or otherwise?"

I thought about Bruno, and about Claude, but neither seemed a likely suspect. Bruno seemed to be on a leash for the moment, and I knew for a fact that Claude was the sort to take matters in his own hands, beside the obvious fact of his current indisposition. Besides, my attacker spoke English like a native.

"No, nothing."

"All right. We'll check the apartment, run down the information on the phone the texts were sent from."

"I appreciate it. It seems like an awful lot of trouble to go to just for a simple assault, Inspector."

He smiled for the first time, a wearily ironic expression. "Normally we wouldn't put these sorts of resources into such a case. But the divisionnaire's wife is a great fan, and he sent word down that every effort was to be made on your behalf."

• • •

Outside the hospital awaited a gauntlet of reporters, print and television, and I was relieved to see Marie-Laure waiting for me by the barrier behind which they stood.

"You lead an interesting life, my friend," she said.

"Lately I do."

"Answer one or two questions as vaguely as possible, then say the whole story's going to be on the network news tomorrow night, right before *Ventura County* comes on."

I stepped out into the throng and tossed out brave, insouciant replies to the questions being shouted at me, then made the announcement as requested. Then, arm in arm with Marie-Laure and not terribly concerned about the effect on her marriage of those clicking cameras and the pictures in tomorrow's papers, I got into the network's waiting car and rode away.

• • •

Marie-Laure wanted to come up to the apartment, but the day had been too exhausting to permit for anything like satisfying intercourse, so I settled for a blowjob in the back of the limo, with Balthazar studiously ignoring us up front. Finished, she zipped me up and bade me good night, and I went upstairs and collapsed onto the bed without even bothering to check what kind of press my beating had earned me.

LUNDI, SEIZE MAI

AS SOON AS I AWOKE I CHECKED THE MAJOR news sites, and they all had a little something, ranging from a dry squib on lemonde.fr mentioning that an actor (unnamed!) from the American soap opera *Ventura County* had been attacked, to *Le Parisien*'s racier coverage, which managed to suggest without coming right out and saying it that I'd been attacked by the irate husband of some seduced woman. The latter site, I was thrilled to see, had posted a picture of me exiting the hospital with a bloody bandage on my temple and another on the back of my neck, a devil-may-care expression on my face. It was a good look for me; I'd have to make a note that somewhere in the film my character should get beaten about the head so he could walk around bloodied but unbowed.

There were more, but none of them told me anything the others hadn't, and only *France-Soir* mentioned my pending interview with the anchor of the evening news (the male anchor, sadly, as his female counterpart was a thing of exquisite beauty with a naughty smirk, and I'd been hoping to meet her). Despite the bountiful heaps of good press, I felt let down for no good reason I could pinpoint, like a spoiled child on Christmas morning who's just realized he's got nothing left to unwrap. After a few moments of stewing I realized what it was: I hadn't seen anything on any of the sites about Claude's disappearance. Loath though I was to admit it, surely the presumed kidnapping by terrorists of one of Europe's wealthiest arms dealers was more newsworthy than my getting brained by an omelette pan.

• • •

To my delight, though, Fred had sent me thirty-five pages of script, about a third of what we'd need for shooting. I opened the file and started reading, and I didn't stop until I'd finished.

It was perfect.

Really funny stuff, plus a decent adventure story with enough twists and turns to allow the audience to forget for a moment that it was watching something as light as Feydeau or Wilde. And a great character for me to play to boot, an exaggerated version of myself, witty, erudite, a devil with the ladies. There were any number of actors who'd kill for a part like this, but it was all mine.

I had to conclude that something about playing the role of jailer had let loose something in Fred's unconscious and let the ideas fly. But this wasn't the work of some idiot savant, letting the words flow through his fingers onto the keys as though via some otherworldly medium; this was the work of a professional, its structure—based on what I could tell from Act I, anyway—classical, its dialogue pitch-perfect. It even had a good part for Esmée. I made a mental note to tell him he needed to write one for Annick, too.

I phoned Marie-Laure and told her the news. "How long until he's finished?"

"I don't know. Not long now, I don't think."

"Hear anything from Claude Guiteau?"

"Not a word on my end," I said. It was the truth, too; last time I saw him he'd had a rubber ball jammed between his jaws.

"Check with that wife of his, will you? I want to know if he's in or out."

"You could just as easily call her yourself."

"I prefer not to. Do it for me, please. And don't forget the interview, I need you in the studio by 5:00 PM."

"I'll be there."

• • •

Ginny called and asked me to log on to her website, giving me a courtesy VIP password so I wouldn't have to enter my credit card information. "I've got some new stuff up, stuff I shot right before I left L.A., you might want to have a look and see if you don't get any ideas."

I logged on and watched her getting her various and sundry orifices penetrated a dozen ways apiece. It all looked fine to me, but it had been a while since I'd had to resort to masturbation for gratification, so I didn't quite know how I was supposed to react. There was one particular clip in which she played an archaeologist who dug up a mummy, which unwrapped his bandages to reveal a still-functioning phallus. Sucking and fucking ensued, and I wondered which of the minor roles in the movie she might be right for.

And then, having exhausted the newer clips, I surfed around the older titles and found one in which she played a bitchy interior decorator ordering around a handyman, who at one point decided he'd had enough, bending her over, tearing her fancy clothes, and giving it to her all kinds of ways until the obligatory facial at the end, with Ginny greedily licking handyman semen off of her cheeks and lips. Something about this one bothered me (and no, it wasn't the implied misogyny—my politics lean leftward but not, as you may have gathered, in the direction of the sexually politically correct).

I watched it again and knew what it was: I'd seen that handyman somewhere before, and not long ago, either.

• • •

After a light lunch of a salad I took a tranquil stroll across the Luxembourg Gardens to our subterranean dungeon to congratulate Fred in person. He was quite pleased with my enthusiasm and outlined his ideas for the next two acts.

"I think I can be done in a week. No, I know I can."

"That's terrific. I'll start getting everything arranged."

"Um." He glanced at the meat locker's large metal doors. "What about our money man?"

I let out a long sigh. There was the fly in the ointment. "I'm working on it. Meanwhile you keep cranking out those pages."

He sat down at the old schoolboy's desk Annick had provided for his use and waved me away, and before I'd gone he was tapping furiously at the keyboard of his laptop.

• • •

In the limo on the way to the studio I remembered where I'd seen the handyman from Ginny's porn video, even came up with his name. He was David Steinke, an actor I'd seen in a couple of L.A. theater productions and whose work had thoroughly impressed me. No wonder I hadn't quite been able to place him—no one expects an actor of that caliber to turn up in a porno. Ginny was another story altogether; her looks were the only thing that had gotten her cast in the first place, and the quality of her work on the show was only a step or two above the level required for porn.

What were the plays I'd seen him in? One was an all-white revival of *Porgy and Bess*, not one of the highlights of L.A. theater of that or any other year but a production in which he himself had excelled. The other was a small piece set in a Louisiana bar involving a gay quadriplegic, a black hit man, and a Klansman who come to mutual understanding and respect during Hurricane Katrina. Steinke's portrayal of the Klansman was sympathetic and nuanced, and I came away from the theater convinced I'd seen a future star.

And of course it had been Ginny who'd accompanied me to both productions. He was a friend of hers from her acting classes and she wanted to support him by bringing as many industry friends as possible to see him at work. The poor guy, he'd given up too easily; nothing legit was open to you once you'd done fuck flicks, Stallone's pre-stardom, one-shot "Italian Stallion" notwithstanding.

"You're quiet tonight," Marie-Laure said.

"Just thinking about someone I used to know who came to a bad end."

"Have you given any thought to what you're going to say?"

"I'm going to say what I told the cops."

She shrugged. "It would be nice if it were something dramatic. Something that suggested a conspiracy."

My cell buzzed. I had a message from Esmée: *MUST SPEAK URGENTLY NOW NOW NOW.*

I put the phone back in my jacket. *"URGENTLY NOW NOW NOW"* from a woman like Esmée meant in reality "I don't want to have to eat dinner by myself" or "Are you with that woman?" And I had the interview to think about.

• • •

The lights of the studio were dim compared to the lights of a set. I was seated across from the anchor during a break, and when the red light came back on we exchanged greetings as though we'd known each other for years. Since we were on the same channel, most viewers would assume that we were old friends. It's absurd, of course, but I've experienced the same thing dozens of times. Once in a gas station in the Rocky Mountains a tiny lady told me she was going to be sure to tell someone named Barney Coggs she'd met me.

"Barney Coggs?" I asked.

She gave me a playful blow on the elbow with the top of her hand. "Our Channel Nine HotNews WeatherCaster!"

"Oh, Barney," I said. "That rascal! Give him my best."

And now I was trying to remember whether the anchor's name was Michel or Daniel. The mnemonic device I'd used had involved a rhyme, and now I was trapped, unable to respond with a casually friendly use of his first name. Ah, well, next time I'd prepare better. I didn't even know how I was going to answer his questions, since the truth as I knew it was pretty thin stuff: Someone sent me a text luring me to an empty apartment, then hit me over the head.

Unfortunately Michel/Daniel had already covered that part of the affair, and it was up to me to elaborate. But I have long been known among my peers as an inspired improviser. Properly speaking, improv isn't simply ad-libbing whatever funny line comes into your head; it's all about propelling a piece forward and giving your fellow improviser something to work with. It's all about trust between performers, and I believed I trusted my interlocutor enough to throw him something he could throw back at me and allow me to further twist it in a way that would surprise and delight our audience.

"Any thoughts as to your attacker's motives?" he asked.

It was as though we'd been working together for years; the question was perfect, and my response was inspired.

"As you know, I've been in Paris working on a film dealing with the theft of art and antiquities. In the course of my research, I've come across a rather unsavory element that has made it quite clear they don't want such a film made."

"Can you specify?"

"I'm afraid I don't have much in the way of specifics. Just that the plot of the script is apparently a bit too close to a certain real-life operation."

"And what makes you certain this attack was related to these characters?"

"I'm not certain. I think that was their idea, to create a certain amount of confusion. I do remember one thing that seemed meaningless at the time, and perhaps it is. But before the second blow, the one that knocked me unconscious, I heard the fellow say, 'Krysmopompas strikes again.' I don't know what it means, if anything."

• • •

I sat in the limo for a minute or two waiting for Marie-Laure to talk on the phone to some network types who were apparently quite pleased with the interview. Even Balthazar wanted to talk about it.

"That's fucked up," he said. "I can't believe you went in there alone and unarmed."

"Yeah, well, I didn't have any reason to think anything was up."

"But you're a celebrity. You should have a bodyguard and shit."

Balthazar struck me both as a tough guy and as a man I could trust, the kind of guy you could ask delicate questions and count on his discretion.

"Balthazar, what would you do if you were in my position? Besides hiring a bodyguard?"

"Shit, man, I'd get me a piece."

"A gun?"

"Shit, yeah."

"I wouldn't know where to go looking for one."

He raised an eyebrow. "I could send you to a guy I know up in Montmartre. You go, you mention you're a friend of mine."

• • •

"That was amazing," Marie-Laure said in the limo as we pulled away from the studio. "I'll be honest, I wasn't sure you were up to an interview on the subject. You seemed so vague and diffident about it. But then you managed to work in the movie and that bullshit about chrysalopolis and art thieves. You know something? I had an orgasm when you said that made-up word. I went right up my spine from my clit to my brain. Say it again."

"Krysmopompas."

A look of feline satisfaction produced itself on her face and she leaned over to whisper in my ear. "I was going to ask whether you wanted champagne and oysters before you fuck me or after, but now I can't wait, so you're going to fuck me in the ladies' room at the restaurant."

"Krysmopompas," I said.

MARDI, DIX-SEPT MAI

I DIDN'T GET HOME UNTIL QUITE LATE, AND I ignored both my mobile and the constantly ringing land line, the latter of which I finally unplugged at three in the morning. I awoke at ten-thirty with Esmée standing over me, the look on her face not unlike that which I imagined Claude might have had on his face the night he tried to shoot me from just about the spot where she now stood.

"Where the fuck is he?"

In my bleary, half-awake state I genuinely had no idea to whom she might be referring. "Where the fuck is who?" I asked.

She slapped me, and she was a lot stronger than I might have guessed looking at her. I swung my legs onto the floor and held my palm to my stinging cheek.

"Do you think I'm stupid? Why didn't you call me back yesterday?"

"I had an interview to do," I said, and I was quite grateful at that moment that the night before I had indeed fulfilled Marie-Laure's fantasy of getting laid in a bathroom stall in a fancy restaurant; I could only imagine how much worse the scene playing out at the moment would have gone for me had another woman been lying there in the bed next to me when Esmée walked in. I don't think it would have led to a threesome.

"I had a visit from the police yesterday. Claude's been kidnapped."

It all came back to me in a horrifying rush, but one thing about being an actor is you learn to seem convincingly surprised at perfectly unsurprising statements. "Kidnapped? Dear God. By whom?"

She slapped me again. "They showed me a picture the kidnappers sent to the press."

Aha. There was the reason the story hadn't broken yet; the cops were keeping it quiet. "A picture," I repeated, an old trick for when you've forgotten your next line and want the other actors in the scene to subtly feed it to you.

"I recognized the baby-blue ball gag, you dumb shit. It's mine—you got it out of the third drawer from the bottom in the armoire."

Damn. She had me there. Still, one had to fight on. "What's this about a ball gag?"

"Give it up. Anyway, even if the ball gag didn't prove it, there you were on TV last night with that 'Krysmopompas' bullshit. I had to call the officer in charge of the case to ask if he'd watched, by the way, just to cover myself. He hadn't, but he's now in touch with the inspector investigating your case. You should be hearing from him today."

"You see, what I was doing there was creating some plausible deniability. I really did get attacked, by the way."

"Look, I'm not mad at you for locking him up, though I'll admit I'm a little hazy on your motivations. What pisses me off is that you didn't tell me right away."

"Really?"

"I wish I'd thought of faking a kidnapping myself. So what's the idea, roughly?" She had calmed down considerably.

I filled her in on Claude's unacceptable behavior and the basics of his captivity, along with the various scenarios that Fred and I had worked out for his eventual release.

"You really didn't think this out at all, did you?" she asked.

"Of course I did. I have multiple scenarios in play, I just haven't settled definitively on any one of them yet."

"The only one that works is this one: We kill him."

"I'm not entirely comfortable with that outcome," I said. This was something of a vast understatement.

"Tell me another that works."

"We release him after a ransom is paid."

"Ransoms are traceable. Besides, he'll kill you."

"He never saw me after he woke up."

"Unless he's brain damaged, he knows it's you. And okay, let's say he's got amnesia, just like one of the characters in your soap opera." (That remark stung a bit, with its implied disrespect aimed at my little corner of the television medium, but I let it pass.) "And let's say he decides to go ahead and finance the movie. What happens when he gets a load of the screenwriter and realizes it's his former jailer?"

A thought did flash into my mind. What if Fred was a look-alike for Claude's captor, perhaps an identical twin? Then I remembered that that had been a plot twist on *Ventura County*. Anticipating her sneering (and absolutely correct) dismissal of the idea, I kept it to myself.

She sat down on the bed next to me, leaned in and kissed me. "If you're worried about the moral aspect of the whole business, I can assure you that Claude is one evil son of a bitch."

"I'm sure he is."

"I've thought about it many times, but I've never really had an opportunity like this one. Think of it. Claude's out of the picture. All that money, mine to control without any interference. We'll make our movie. We can be seen together in public without fear of Claude having one or both of us killed."

It was all sounding pretty good to me. I have nothing against money, and though I wasn't exactly lacking for it at the moment, I didn't have Claude Guiteau's kind of money, not by a long shot, and having a girlfriend with that kind of dough was the next best thing. And then she said something that made my blood run cold:

"After a decent interval we can get married."

• • •

Even an unwanted marriage proposal seems to call for a celebratory fuck, and after we were finished we showered together and she left. Less than a half an hour later I answered the door to find Inspector Bonnot, of the Police Judiciaire, who was displeased that I'd revealed a piece of important evidence in a TV interview without having told him.

"This Krysmopompas fellow, you have any idea who he is?"

"No, and I'm sorry I didn't mention it to you when you debriefed me, it was something I suddenly recalled yesterday afternoon. I meant to call you and fill you in, I really did."

He grilled me for a while and I invented a few small details that seemed to please him.

"I'm surprised you have so much time to spend on a simple assault and battery," I said.

"As I told you before, the divisionnaire's wife is a big fan. And don't assume that yours is an isolated case," he said. "Was there any context to this Krysmopompas comment? Did he indicate whether Krysmopompas was a group, or perhaps just a *nom de crime* he'd dreamed up?"

"Nothing like that, sir," I said, "just the word."

"It's a funny word. I'm surprised you remembered it, having only heard it once. Are you sure you got it right?" He was quite friendly in his interrogation, nothing insinuating about it. I was making little mental notes the whole time in case I ever got to play a cop.

"I'm an actor, Captain, accustomed to memorizing quickly and exactly. What's it mean, anyway?"

"We're working on that now," he said.

• • •

Late in the day I smuggled Esmée down to see her husband, and Fred damn near swallowed his chewing gum at the sight of her.

"Let's have a look," she said.

"Are you sure you want him seeing you?"

"Who cares? He's good as dead."

This didn't go over very well with Fred, who was still laboring under the misconception that somehow this was going to end with Claude free and bearing us no ill will. I was a bit ashamed at my capacity for self-delusion, which had allowed me to entertain that same absurd notion until disabused of it by Esmée's coldhearted but absolutely logical and undeniable dissection of the situation. I suppose on some unconscious level I knew from the moment I brought the statue down on his head that at some point I was going to have to finish him off, and oddly enough the notion that I would have to serve as Claude's executioner came as a relief, now that Esmée was in the loop.

As Fred sputtered an incomprehensible protest, I opened the massive door to the meat locker. The stench from within was eye-watering, but Esmée stood impassive in the doorway and stared at her husband with one eyebrow arched and one hand on her beautiful hip.

Still bound to his chair, stripped now to his boxer shorts and undershirt, hair disheveled and face black and blue (from a number of falls he'd taken while trying to sleep sitting up), dried spittle caked on his chin, he looked up at Esmée. At first his eyes showed confusion, then hope, and finally hatred and rage as he understood that she was not there for purposes of ransom or rescue. He snarled unintelligibly through the ball gag and strained ineffectively against the ropes, which I now saw that Fred had tightened too far; his hands were a dull shade of purple.

"I told you that fucking ball gag was too big," she said to him. "Not too comfortable for long-term wear, is it?"

He was roaring so fiercely I began to fear he was going to choke on his own saliva, struggling so hard I thought he might break the solid old wooden chair.

"I'd kiss you," she said, "but you smell like shit, dear." She turned to me. "Better shut him in again. The sight of me is going to give him a heart attack, and the police are going to expect a proper execution-style slaying from the likes of Krysmopompas."

That was when Claude first turned his attention to me. After a momentary escalation of his rage, he started laughing, at least as far as that was possible with an enormous blue rubber ball in his mouth.

"What were you thinking, Claude?" she asked. "Trying to kill him on Friday the thirteenth? Don't you know that's an unlucky day?" Then she pulled me to her and kissed me, and while I normally would have shown poor Claude some consideration by stopping there, there was something about Esmée that made me follow her lead, and pretty soon we were practically dry-humping right there in front of him. Then, laughing, she slammed the meat locker door shut.

"That was fun," she said.

"I hadn't realized before that you actually disliked him," I said. "I thought you just had a wandering eye."

"I've hated him since before we were married. I can't wait to kill him."

That was when I noticed that Fred was softly weeping at his keyboard. "I don't want to kill him."

"No choice now, old chum," I said. "He knows us."

"You don't understand. I've taken care of him. Fed him. Cleaned up his messes. I'm a little bit attached to him."

"For God's sake, he's not a baby bird you rescued," Esmée said. "He's an arms dealer, responsible for the deaths of a hundred thousand innocents."

Fred nodded, eyes down. Poor guy was lonely, and here I'd provided him with someone to take care of, and suddenly I was yanking that person away to be shot, just like Old Yeller. I remembered now somewhat shamefacedly that I'd promised to get him laid and then ignored my duty as a friend.

"Say, Esmée, you don't happen to know any attractive gals who might want to hook up with a talented young writer about to hit the big time?"

She looked him over and shrugged. "If a guy's in show business, most girls will fuck anybody. Sure, I'll set him up with somebody."

Fred was looking a little better. "Actually, I'm thirty-two, not all that young."

And then Annick stepped in out of the darkness of the old abandoned kitchen, shocked and, I think, a little angry at the sight of Esmée. "What the fuck is she doing here?"

"Didn't expect to see me, did you, dear?" Esmée said with a smile that frightened me more than her suggestion of marriage had.

"Has he seen her?" Annick wanted to know.

"He has," I said.

"Then he's a dead man, isn't he?"

"Looks that way from my perspective."

Annick let out a long, deep breath, half of angry frustration and half of resignation. "This is going to open me up to all kinds of weird emotional shit with Bruno," she said.

"So don't tell him," Esmée suggested with a shrug.

• • •

That night I brought Ginny out to dinner with Casselini, the director, and suggested he might want to cast her in the small but crucial role of Esmeralda, the peasant girl who helps my character hide the arms while he's being chased by a neo-Nazi biker gang in the employ of the mad art collector. Casselini couldn't stop staring at Ginny's tits, provocatively displayed as they were in a combination of Miracle Bra and low-necked top. Professional that she was, his attentions bothered her not a whit.

"Like 'em?" she asked. "They're real. If you want we could go into the bathroom and have a squeeze."

"That's probably not such a great idea," I told her, though Casselini seemed quite keen on it.

"Why not?" she said. "You said you fucked that network lady in a restaurant crapper, and I bet that was a nicer place than this."

I had to allow that both her points were well taken, and between courses she got up and went to the ladies' room. After a decent interval Casselini did the same, and five minutes later they were both back at the table.

I listened to him rhapsodize about her beauty for the rest of the dinner, and we agreed that she was perfect for the role. She gave him the password for free entry and downloads on her site, as well as her cell number.

We walked back to her hotel again. I wasn't normally that much into the long after-dinner promenades, but with Ginny it was just about the only way to have a conversation that wasn't postcoital, since the minute you entered a room alone with her was usually her signal that the fucking was to commence.

"Did you get a chance to look at the site?"

"I did. Very impressive. You're making good coin?"

"You have no idea. Monthly memberships, day passes, automatic rebilling. Plus I've got three clip sites where guys who don't want to join up can just pay for individual downloads."

"Three clip sites?"

"One's me with guys, one's me with guys and gals, the other I'm a dominatrix."

"You? Really?"

"Don't sound so surprised. I'm a pretty good actress, you said so yourself."

We were stopped by a pair of young men, autograph seekers, and to my surprise it wasn't mine but hers they wanted.

"Please," one of them said in perfect English. "Let your bush grow back."

"Sorry," she said. "It's what the market demands at the moment."

The other one agreed. "Bald pussy is for squares. And your bush is so perfect and blond."

"Try an experiment," the first one said. "Do a series wearing a merkin and see how sales go."

"I just may do that. Thanks for the input, fellas."

She kissed each of them on the cheek and they were on their way. "What's a merkin?" I asked.

"Pubic wig. From back in the days when people's body hair used to fall out from smallpox and they didn't want their lovers to know they'd had it."

We walked for a minute or two in silence, and then she asked me if something was bothering me.

"Just wondering how a couple of French kids knew a word in English that I didn't. And an Elizabethan one at that."

• • •

The desk clerk at the hotel was very excited to see us. "The manager on duty before me made a grave error in judgment," he said. "I'm afraid, madame, he allowed your husband access to your suite."

For a moment Ginny was stupefied, then alarmed. "My husband? I don't have a husband anymore."

"He had a valid American passport, listing you as his spouse. The manager in question will be in a great deal of trouble for this."

"There's no point to that," I said. "It was an honest mistake. The question is, what do we do now? Call the police?"

"It would be a delicate matter," the night clerk said. "Potentially embarrassing for the hotel."

"Why don't you go up there and tell him to take a flying fuck at the moon," she said to me. "He's a shrimp, you could take him on easy."

I looked at the night clerk seeking his approval. He nodded, though he looked far from certain that this was actually the best plan.

• • •

She was staying on the seventh floor in a suite fit for royalty. I slid the card into the lock and it clicked open, then swung the door quietly open. I heard the sound of a shower running and what sounded like a woman singing to herself. Had this ex-husband actually had the balls to bring a woman up to Ginny's room? I supposed, though, once you've been married to a porn star your notions of propriety probably change somewhat.

Cautiously I moved into the suite's front room, and as I rounded the corner I came face-to-face with a tall woman, heavily made up, wearing a dressing gown with a towel wrapped

Lana Turner–like in a turban around her hair. Gathering the front of the dressing gown protectively together, she let loose a shriek loud enough to draw my hands to my ears, and then she punched me.

To say I wasn't expecting the punch is one thing; it's quite another to express my surprise at its force. It was, without a doubt, a man's fist, and when I hit back I assumed I was hitting a man. What makeup came off on my fist revealed a fine skein of whiskers on a strong jaw, and when he was down I kicked him hard in the jaw, which didn't stop him. He lunged for my throat and plunged both thumbs into my trachea, and I thought he might be strong enough to choke me into unconsciousness.

So I went for his left eye, one thumb on the nasal corner and the other at the distal. As soon as I applied the smallest amount of pressure he screamed at the pain—a very male sound, compared with the shriek my entry had provoked—and rolled off of me.

"You son of a bitch," he said, and I knew that voice right away. The dressing gown was open now to reveal a pair of panties and matching bra, both of which I recognized as Ginny's, the turban lay wet on the floor, and he sprinted for the front door and bolted down the hall to the stairwell. There wasn't any point in chasing him; I didn't want him arrested anyway. Even underneath the exaggerated makeup I now recognized him, and I had plans for him.

• • •

"You never told me you were married to David Steinke," I said when I got Ginny up to the room.

"Yeah, it didn't last long. Kind of a mistake. He didn't like me doing the vids with other guys, just wanted me to make them with him. Problem was the ones he wanted to do were just too damn kinky."

"Some of the ones I saw were pretty far out."

"Yeah, but his were real specific kinks most guys don't share. Rubber glove fetish, diaper play, that kind of shit. I mean, there's a market for everything, but I'm in porn to make money, not satisfy some obscure niche for the kind of weirdos who don't even get off on regular porn."

"By the way, he made off with your dressing gown and a matching set of bra and panties."

"By 'made off with,' I assume you mean 'ran away wearing'?"

"Basically, yeah."

"Huh. For him cross-dressing is usually a prelude to either fisting or some serious scat-play, so it's a good thing you chased him off."

"You know how you might reach him if you needed to?"

"Probably," she said. "Why?"

"No reason."

• • •

Having been treated to a hero's repertoire of arcane sexual favors from a very grateful Ginny, I left the hotel and, wearing a cap and dark glasses and carrying a newspaper, got onto the Métro.

I was standing across a lady with one clouded, milky eye and a cane and who looked too old to be out and about that late. She reminded me of my great-grandmother who died when I was five, a dear old soul who always smelled of violets and tooth decay and who thought the sun shone out my little ass. She seemed ancient to me, and I suppose she must have been past ninety when she finally went. The sudden memory of her holding me in her lap and handing me a hard candy wrapped in cellophane made me chuckle, which drew the attention of the old lady across the aisle from me.

"Filth," she said, little flecks of spit flying from her false teeth. "Pervert."

I looked around to see who she was talking about. Was she referring to me, or to Dr. Crandall Taylor, or had she mistaken me, with my dark glasses and baseball cap with its bill pulled down, for Satan or his emissary?

"You there," she said, fixing her milky gaze on me. "You heard me. I know all about you and your filthy, filthy games. People like you ruin this life for decent folk like me and Raymond."

I looked away, hoping whatever her particular brand of crazy was would allow her to fix her rage on someone else, but she kept it up until she got off at Poissonières. As she struggled to get onto the platform before the closing of the doors I heard her say, "Yes, Raymond, I told the dirty little bastard."

• • •

I got out at Pigalle, crossed the square, and mounted the rue Germain Pilon. As I reached the top someone called out to me.

"Want a date?" rasped a feminine voice trying desperately to rise above its unmistakably masculine natural register. Across from me stood a streetwalker who looked like Yaphet Kotto in drag.

"Thanks anyway," I said, wondering why tonight seemed to be drag queen night in Paris and wondering also who exactly constituted the clientele for his genre of hooker. There was a market for any kind, I supposed; there used to be a block—maybe there still is—at the south end of the rue St. Denis where all the whores were over sixty; one or two of them were quite elegant ladies, but most were weather-beaten alcoholics catering to the poorest, most indigent of johns. I remember passing through on my way to the Les Halles RER station one day, I must have been about twenty, when someone hissed at me.

"*Jeune homme!*" An obese crone of seventy-odd years was leering at me from a doorway. "*Viens voir!*" Then she hiked up her skirt to reveal an immense, ancient salt-and-pepper bush above a pair of chalky thighs, withered and dimpled. When I failed to approach, she tilted her head down at her crotch and grinned, nodding. "*Viens voir!*" Though I declined the invitation, I have no doubt that she did a lively trade on the whole.

• • •

I said earlier I wasn't going to complain about being a celebrity, and I'm not, but here's where I point out that this is one of those situations where it complicates things. In L.A. you just go to the store and say, "I'd like a gun, please, and some armor-piercing bullets, and throw in one of those maps to the Stars' Homes while you're at it," and no one bats an eye. In Paris you have to know someone who knows someone, and if you're famous then it's damned hard for word not to get around that you bought a gun.

I should have had Fred do it, but he was busy taking care of Claude, and I was impatient for the script to be finished. Anyway, on the Place des Abbesses I found the café Balthazar had mentioned, and at the bar I ordered a Kanterbräu and asked for Gégé.

"Never heard of him," the bartender said.

"I'm a friend of Balthazar's."

"I don't know any Balthazar."

I could understand his reluctance to help. Here was a guy with a baseball cap and dark glasses—indoors, at midnight—and a foreign accent, asking for someone who does a brisk trade in various sorts of illegal merchandise in your place of business. He must have taken me for some sort of cop, and reluctant though I was to drop my cover, I took off my shades for a moment.

"I'm not a cop," I said. "More like a doctor."

Recognizing me, he nodded and poured me a beer. "Okay. Balthazar said you might come by. I'm Gégé. What you need?"

"Something for protection."

"I got it." He yelled at a young man in a black waiter's vest who was sweeping around the pinball machine. "Ahmed, watch the bar for a minute."

• • •

The gun was in a safe in the office, and he put on a pair of latex gloves before he took it out. He handed me a pair and advised me to put them on.

"Why?"

"Because I don't have any prints on this gun and neither should you. Last guy who handled this gun is an asshole, and if anything funny happens we don't want it traced to us, do we?"

"I just want it for protection."

"I don't give a shit why you want it. I'm just offering you some advice. Wear the gloves when you handle the gun and I promise you'll be happy about it later."

MERCREDI, DIX-HUIT MAI

2:00 AM.
I was at home in a very deep and contented sleep when I was awakened by an indignant Esmée.

"What are you doing asleep?" she asked.

"It's been a pretty big day, actually." I didn't mention the fist-fight with the cross dresser or the strenuous sex with said tranny's estranged wife, as this wasn't the kind of information that would soothe Esmée, but I did allow as how I'd purchased a gun for self-defense.

"Excellent," she said. "It's going to be a big night, too. Come on, get dressed."

I was hoping the big night wasn't going to involve more than one ejaculation, since I'd already done that twice and was approaching my limit. "Can whatever it is wait until morning?"

"Tonight's the night. Claude's last."

Shit. Despite the purchase of the gun I hadn't thought about its eventual use all night, really, which was sort of a blessing. My ability to compartmentalize has been a boon to me as an actor; no matter what turmoil is affecting my personal life, I'm always in the moment onstage or on set. "You know, I'm pretty beat. Could we do it tomorrow?"

"Get out of bed. It's tonight."

I got out of bed and got dressed without showering, presuming that she wouldn't be too keen on my taking the time for it. In the kitchen I ate an apple to make me alert (better than coffee, at least in my case), and I let her leave first in case we were spotted.

Ten minutes later I left the building myself and, as luck would have it, hanging around outside the nightclub next door was the guy I'd beaten up the week previous. He looked just as drunk as he had that night, and he stared at me with a look of intense but befuddled concentration while his buddies laughed at him.

I turned the corner in a hurry and caught up with Esmée's mint-condition '67 Karmann Ghia a few hundred meters up the Boulevard St. Germain. With her at the wheel we raced down the near-empty boulevard over to the Cluny and then up the Boulevard St. Michel while she lectured me about taking things more seriously. Then she admitted that my ability to face such a situation with aplomb, even boredom, was one of the things that drove her mad with desire. I didn't have the heart to tell her that my attitude wasn't insouciance or indifference or anything of the sort; it was just sexual exhaustion, ascribable to one of her rivals.

We drove well past the dormitory, all the way up to the Boulevard du Port-Royal, where she parked on the sidewalk and we walked down a side street to where a baker's truck sat. She pulled out a set of keys and we drove it in silence to the rue de l'Abbé de l'Épée.

• • •

The mood in the basement was dismal, funereal even. Annick and Fred had been drinking wine and were both telling sad tales of love gone wrong, and before we got started with the main business of the night, Esmée joined in.

"Wait until you're older," Esmée said. "Believe me, whatever heartbreaks you've had you'll have worse before you're through."

"I don't know," I said. "Seems to me the main thing is not to take these things so seriously and just try and have fun."

All three of them looked at me as though I were an idiot or a bastard, but I was the only one of the four of us not whining about long-gone, unfaithful lovers. Hadn't I ever had my heart broken? Sure I had; the difference was that after a brief period of sadness I stopped giving a shit. And that's why, romantically speaking, I am one of the happiest sons of bitches you will ever encounter.

After five minutes of listening to them I realized that Esmée was no longer in command, that in the presence of the others she was deferring to my authority. So I told them to knock it off. It was time to transport Claude. When we opened the door to the meat locker and turned on the light he squealed through the gag at the sight of Esmée, or more precisely at her predatory expression, and when he saw that steamer trunk we were going to put him in he panicked and began struggling for real. Weak though he was from nearly a week in restraints, the fear of death stimulated his adrenal glands and I thought he was going to bust that chair into pieces.

"For God's sake, be a man," Esmée said. That was a bit harsh given the circumstance, but I didn't want to have to fight him into the trunk. So I went into another part of the old kitchen carrying a flashlight and grabbed a big cast-iron skillet off the wall.

When I came back he was still thrashing, wide-eyed, and the chair had fallen over on its side. I knocked him unconscious with a single blow and then with some revulsion stuffed his nearly nude, barely breathing body into the trunk and locked it. It was harder this time, perhaps because of the smell of him, and in any case a great deal more difficult than the movie I mentioned earlier would have suggested.

The mood in the bread truck was oddly jolly, as though the four of us were on our way to the Bois de Boulogne for a picnic or a day at Longchamp instead of a murder and a body dump. Esmée and Annick were telling stories about their respective adolescent forays into sexual experimentation, and Fred took advantage of a conversational tangent in the direction of zoophilia to describe one of the many subplots of the novel he'd interrupted in order to work on the movie.

"This guy's in love with a dog," he said, and he got a little incensed when the girls laughed. "No, it's a serious examination of the emotion. What does it mean when a man loves, fully and completely, his neighbor's German shepherd?"

More gales of raucous laughter, followed by more rationalizing, followed by more laughter, until finally Fred himself joined in.

"Maybe you could have the dog fall in love with a cat," Annick said. "A triangle is always interesting."

I looked in the back where she and Fred were seated and I couldn't help noticing that she was sitting closer to him than the limitations of space necessarily dictated, and I felt good for both of them. Fred needed a woman, and a young and beautiful one would turn his morbid attention away from his ex-wife; in addition it was difficult to see how Annick could stay in a relationship with Bruno now that she was a giggling accomplice in his father's murder.

We drove the bread truck some distance into the park, past vast empty spaces and patches crowded with whores and johns, past Longchamp racetrack until finally, having driven such a circuitous, labyrinthine route that I wasn't sure I could have found my way out alone, we stopped. There was no one in sight, and the four of us unloaded the trunk and carried it into the woods.

Someone had dumped a load of old television sets there in the middle of the Bois. I shone my flashlight around and counted more than thirty of them, their round, green glass picture tubes shattered. They all looked to date back to the 1970s at least, and I thought it would make an interesting publicity shot, me standing before all those derelict televisions in the Bois at night, but before Fred could snap a picture with my little Canon Annick reminded us quite rightly that we didn't want to be connected to the spot, in terms of evidence.

I unlocked the trunk and dumped Claude on the ground. He was starting to come around, and the subject came up for the first time of who was to commit the crime itself, and in what manner.

Esmée wanted to tie a noose around his neck and attach it to his feet so that he would slowly strangle himself, but I pointed out that this might take a while and we didn't have the time to stick around and make sure he was dead before some passerby noticed him. She pouted but admitted that I was right, to the obvious relief of Annick and Fred, neither of whom was entirely sanguine about the prospect of having to watch such a death. I have to admit I didn't like the idea much either, even taking into account Claude's crimes against humanity. So I extracted from my inside jacket pocket the very pair of latex gloves Gégé had given me, and then I grabbed the gun and placed it against Claude's temple and fired.

The others stood there in stunned silence, and I ran to the pile of televisions and threw up inside the chassis of an old Thomson, through its shattered glass screen.

After a minute or so Fred spoke up. "Maybe we should leave in case someone heard the shot."

"Shots go off here all the time," Esmée said, but she was moving in the direction of the bread truck. Fred and I took the trunk and followed.

• • •

We drove in silence through Boulogne-Billancourt and I told Esmée to stop on the Pont de St. Cloud. I got out and, still wearing my blood-spattered latex gloves, tossed the gun into the Seine. I had spent the exorbitant sum of five hundred euros on it, double what it was probably really worth, and it seemed a shame to be letting it go after only a few short hours of ownership and a single shot fired, but that was the way it was.

• • •

The first order of business was to drop Esmée off at her Karmann Ghia so she could be at home when the police called. Fred took the wheel and we left the bread truck where Esmée had picked it up, and I tossed the bloody latex gloves into a storm drain. Then we repaired on foot to the basement of the dormitory where we spent a good deal of time removing any traces of Claude's captivity there. In the meantime Annick was kind enough to take my bloodied shirt upstairs and wash it in the laundry room. By the time it was clean and dried, Fred and I had done a pretty good job on the meat locker, to which only the faintest odor still clung. He and I left on foot via the rear entryway while Annick went upstairs to sleep.

It was almost five in the morning, but neither Fred nor I was sleepy. We walked down to the river and crossed the bridge onto the Île de la Cité and proceeded to walk its periphery twice before heading over to the Île St. Louis for more mindless circular wandering. We'd been at it for more than half an hour before Fred finally spoke.

"Is that the first time you ever killed someone?" he asked.

"It was, but it wasn't the first time I ever tried."

He let that one lie, and we made another half-orbit of the island before he spoke again. "It didn't bother me as much as I thought it would."

"Does that worry you?"

"Not especially."

"You know, I think Annick's developed a soft spot for you."

"Annick?" He sounded pleased but disbelieving. "She's beautiful. And twenty-three. What does she want with a guy like me?"

"Don't sell yourself short. You're a writer, and on the verge of being a very successful one. And I think she saw qualities in you this last week that she admired. She saw you nurturing, taking care of another human being, and becoming emotionally connected to that person despite the circumstances."

"You really think she's interested?"

"Fred, there are lots of subjects where you can safely ignore anything I have to say. But where women are concerned, you can take it to the bank."

He didn't answer, or look back at me, but spent the rest of our walk lost in happy reverie.

• • •

Fred and I went our separate ways shortly after the sun rose—his mood having markedly improved to the point that he was almost giddy—and upon my return to the apartment I showered and quickly thereafter fell into a deep, refreshing sleep that was not interrupted until well past noon by the doorbell. I threw on a clean pair of pants and shirt and opened the door to a lugubrious Inspector Bonnot, who entered the apartment unbidden.

"Can I offer you some coffee?" I asked him.

"Unnecessary," he said. "Did you hear from Mme. Guiteau yesterday?"

Which day was yesterday? My sleep schedule was so far out of joint that I wasn't sure, but assuming that the answer was supposed to be yes, I said I had. Then it struck me that I didn't know whether she was supposed to have confided in me or not about the kidnapping. Pretending I didn't know about the affair seemed more dangerous than frank curiosity, though, and I acted accordingly. "She was distraught about her husband's abduction. If there's anything I can do to help, Inspector—"

"Claude Guiteau is dead. Executed."

Once again, feigning shock is one of those things that separate the real actor from the hammy amateur. The latter will let his jaw fall open, ask when, my God, how? it's so unfair, et cetera. He'll look away, maybe at the ground, maybe into the distance, shake his head, all kinds of histrionic crap. I just stared the inspector in the eye.

"Holy shit," I said. "You're fucking kidding."

"Not in the slightest. I assume Mme. Guiteau also told you that his kidnappers used the name Krysmopompas in their communications with the press."

"She said something like that. I thought she must have had it wrong."

"What was the nature of your business with M. Guiteau?"

"I was trying to get him to invest in a film. His wife is an actress."

"Yes," Bonnot said in a tone that suggested he wasn't entirely convinced of the legitimacy of Mme. Guiteau's acting career. "So she says as well."

"She was in a Dutch film last year that got good notices," I said.

He grunted and shrugged. "And M. Guiteau, did he seem favorably disposed toward financing this film of yours?"

"It was hard for me to say. Esmée—Mme. Guiteau—kept telling me he was all for it, but I only met him once, and since then he's been out of the country."

"Not quite. He reentered Europe via Lisbon over a week ago, and according to his business associates he wasn't heard from after that. You know what he did for a living, I presume."

"I know he had his fingers in a lot of pies, but mostly he was an arms dealer, according to Esmée."

"You're also acquainted with his son Bruno."

"I met him once or twice."

He looked up from his file. "Kid says you beat the shit out of him in his father's nightclub. Is that right?"

"He attacked me and I defended myself."

"He attacked you. Any particular reason?"

Again a dilemma: to cop to the fact that I was fucking Bruno's girl or risk getting caught in a lie. "He found out I was screwing his girlfriend."

Bonnot nodded. "I wasn't sure it was true, but that's what he told me. So that's how you got mixed up with all these people?"

"More or less."

"He's also quite jealous of his stepmother. Claims they had a two-year affair he's never quite gotten over."

"Really?" I didn't have to pretend to be surprised. Somehow I'd assumed that Esmée had been cockteasing the boy all along, but the idea of her actually taking her husband's son to bed was off-putting to say the least.

"And he's not the only one jealous of Mme. Guiteau. His father was convinced that she was screwing someone, and Bruno thinks it was you."

"Inspector, I'm nothing if not a careerist. I'll fuck just about any attractive woman between the ages of sixteen and seventy, but when it stands in the way of getting a movie made I go home, as you say, *la bite sous le bras*. Anyway, I'm involved with a couple of other women at the moment and they keep me busy."

"So I understand. I looked at your girlfriend's website."

"Ginny. Yeah, she's quite a number."

"So she is. The night man at her hotel had an interesting story, incidentally, about you chasing an intruder out of her suite last night."

My God, was that just last night? "Some fellow got the key by claiming to be her ex-husband. Did you talk to her?"

"She says she didn't get upstairs until you'd already chased him away."

"That's right. Presumably a deranged fan," I said.

"Presumably," he said, looking down at his notes. "One more thing before I go. Would it be too much to ask for a signed photograph?"

"For the wife of the divisionnaire? Certainly." I rose to get one and he spoke again.

"Actually, I'd like three, if you don't mind. My wife and daughter, you see. . . ." He shrugged and, for the first time in my presence, smiled.

In my briefcase I carry a stack of different glossies—in costume as Dr. Crandall dressed for surgery, another dressed for the doctor's hobby, polo, and a head shot wearing a tuxedo and a smoky, jaded look. I signed all three, personalized them for each lady in question, and bade the inspector goodbye.

• • •

The murder was all over the news, and now that Claude was dead, that photograph Fred had taken was on every paper's front page and website. Esmée called me to inform me that in addition to the official funeral, which would be attended in the hundreds and heavily covered by the media, a private memorial would be held the next night for close friends and family at the Hanoi Hilton, and she hoped I'd attend. Perhaps I'd like to bring my friend the porn star, she suggested without the least hint of malice in her voice, which clued me in to the fact that she thought the phone might be bugged.

"I'll bring her if she's available," I said.

• • •

While I ate my lunch—a green salad with a macédoine and some smoked salmon—Marie-Laure called, distraught at the news.

"What does this mean for the film?" she asked.

"I haven't really thought it through," I said. "I suppose it'll be up to Esmée. Of course I don't know how much money he really had, or what shape the estate will be in once it's settled. And widowhood may dampen Esmée's burning desire for stardom."

That was bullshit, of course. Nothing, least of all the death of Claude, was going to diminish Esmée's ambitions.

"Yes, you're right," Marie-Laure said. "It's too soon to know anything, isn't it?"

"I feel like a rat even talking about it so soon after."

"Don't be an asshole," she said. "Want to see me tonight?"

"I don't know. I didn't get much sleep last night, I was thinking I might stay in."

"Don't lie to me. Look, I'm married, right? I'm spoken for. I get it, you fuck other women, and I really don't care. But don't lie to me, okay? That pisses me off."

The irritation in her voice turned me on. There's nothing like sex tinged with a little hostility, so I agreed to meet her at eight o'clock for a drink and dinner.

• • •

I wandered down to Fred's bookstore in search of something diverting, not really knowing whether Fred would be there or not. He was, and given the state he was in, I was glad he hadn't called.

"The police were here," he said.

"Okay. What did you tell them?"

"Nothing. They wanted to know why I hadn't been in to work all week."

I hadn't even considered Fred's day job when I assigned him to guard duty, and I wondered now whether I shouldn't reimburse him for his lost wages. Probably not, since that would likely complicate any future case that might be made against us, not to mention the movie deal. "What did you say?"

"I said I was working on the script. Which was true. They wanted to see it."

"Did you let them?"

"I told them I'd have to ask you first."

"Good for you. Well, it's all right with me if they want to have a look. Any idea how they got the idea to talk to you?"

"From Marie-Laure. They wanted to know about anybody associated with this film project."

"Hmm. I wonder why that is."

Fred seemed genuinely distressed by my failure to add things up. His voice went up an octave and his eyes fairly popped out of their orbits. "Why? Because it's the only thing linking the two Krysmopompas cases."

"Oh." Trust a writer to make that leap. I should have consulted with him at every stage of the affair, though to be fair the whole business had been improvised and markedly free of any careful planning. In retrospect it was a miracle we'd gotten this far. "Maybe Krysmopompas needs to strike again."

He shook his head, in disbelief rather than as a negation of my suggestion. "You're insane."

"Look, it's great publicity. Maybe we could write this Krysmopompas into the script."

"No. Krysmopompas needs to disappear."

"Ah, but if he disappears right after Guiteau dies, doesn't that make it seem as though he or they were just a cover for someone with a grudge against him?"

He nodded, thinking hard. Being detail oriented probably helps when plotting out books and movies, but in daily life it seems to add to the stress.

"Meanwhile what's the word with Annick?" I asked.

"Nothing."

"For Christ's sake, give her a call. She's not going to do all the work, she's a girl." Of course she'd been plenty aggressive with me, but I was a celebrity, and the rules were different.

"I don't have her number," he said, looking very much like the kind of guy who never gets the kind of woman he really wants because he convinces himself he's not worthy.

I wasn't buying it. "Give me your cell phone," I said, and when he reluctantly handed it over I programmed Annick's number into it and hit DIAL, then handed it back to him as it started ringing. Then I slapped him on the shoulder and left.

• • •

At Palais Royal I picked up my usual assortment of newspapers and sat down in a café to do the *Herald Tribune*'s crossword puzzle. There was a major story about poor Claude on the front page above the fold, but I'd had enough of that for a while.

Having finished the top and bottom of the puzzle, I got stuck, as was often the case on one of the clues in the middle, and having been interrupted no fewer than four times by fans—two of whom sought medical advice, and only one of whom sympathetically mentioned my injury—I turned on my phone to check my e-mail. The only one of any significance was from my agent:

> *The role on Blindsided went to Dean Flax, the worst actor of his generation, who will thus be making money for his agent and increasing his visibility. The gig was yours if you wanted it and I couldn't even get you to show up for the audition. This is it, pal, the end of the line. I wash my hands of the whole business.*
> *—Ted*

I composed a quick reply:

> *Nice hearing from you, Bunny. Attached are some news articles about me. They're in French but someone in the office should be able to translate. What do you think? I've been targeted by the same terrorists who killed this famous arms dealer here (more articles attached, but the L.A. Times should have something too). He was the investor in my movie, which should have you salivating at all the possibilities. I know you had your heart set on me as third or fourth banana on your crappy network show, but trust me when I say this movie is going to do boffo business over here. If you can forgive me I will shortly have contracts for you to negotiate. Why don't you come on over and have yourself a little vacation?*

I didn't really care whether he kept me on or not; the fact that he was so ready to drop me as a client after a single missed audition was hurtful, and since I'd come to France my career was going great guns without his help. But we'd been friends for a long time, and he'd helped me out in my hungry early days in Hollywood, and in the end I decided to leave it up to him.

I went back to the puzzle. The clue that was vexing me, 27 Across, was nebulous: "Protozoans in low places." I had an *m* and a *v* and an *l*, but the surrounding Down clues told me nothing, and without 27 Across I would be struggling with the damned thing all afternoon.

I called Fred, and he picked up on the first ring, the panic rising steadily in his voice. "What is it?"

"Relax, it's just a crossword problem." I laid it out for him, and I could feel him calming down on the other end as he pondered it.

"Try 'Trichomonas vaginalis,' if that's not too many letters."

It fit perfectly, and suddenly the intersecting Down clues made sense. "Thanks, pal. Your repertoire of obscure facts is pretty amazing."

"It's not that obscure. In fact . . ."

"Listen, I gotta go. How soon before we have a finished script?"

"Soon. I'm cranking through the thing."

"Good. Keep me posted. We've got some momentum despite it all, let's get it made."

"Right, chief," he said, and he hung up.

• • •

Marie-Laure and I settled on sushi in a little place near Les Halles. We sat at the bar and watched the chef at work, and it turned out that Marie-Laure wasn't quite as adventurous in the sashimi department as she had implied. She bristled at the sight of the sea urchin, which to me is the heart of any sushi meal, and stuck mostly to freshwater eel (smoked) and various rolls. I didn't tease her about it, sensing that the ends I sought would be more easily met via other means.

"Script's almost done," I told her as we neared the end of the meal. It was time to talk some business, as it was the network paying for dinner.

"Wonderful. Have you spoken to Esmée?"

"Not since the police told her about her husband."

"When are you going to see her?"

"There's a memorial tomorrow at the Hanoi Hilton, if you want to come along with me."

She sniffed, an almost imperceptible note of jealousy clinging to the sound. "I would have thought you'd want your porn star on your arm. Anyway, shouldn't we be thinking of getting you a bodyguard? Who knows when this Krystalvision or Kriskringle or whatever he's called is going to come after you again."

"I really hate the idea of being surrounded by goons," I said, smiling kindly at a half-crippled old lady limping across the dining room for an autograph and possibly a diagnosis. "I like the idea that my fans can get to me."

"Suit yourself," she said, and turned her attention to the remainder of her California roll as I began conversing with the pain-wracked senior. The old dear didn't want medical advice and in fact wanted to discuss my methods of preparation. She was a stage actress herself, with a number of film roles to her credit, and she had admired my work. I was delighted at the chance to talk shop with an old pro, and as we spoke I started thinking about whether or not there was a part for her in the movie. Perhaps an elderly shepherdess who leads our man to safety. Of course I'd have to consult with Fred about altering or adding a character, but I didn't think that would be too much to ask.

When she waddled back to her own table, Marie-Laure spoke up. "You know who that was?"

"She's an actress."

"She used to be. She jumped out of the window of her apartment over a married politician who stopped returning her calls. She'd been out on the balcony for hours before she finally jumped."

"Wow."

"Yeah, wow. So of course there were TV cameras, and everybody saw the jump. She hasn't worked since, she's completely bonkers." She leaned over to whisper the tragic end of her story: "She thinks she's still a star."

On the way to Marie-Laure's apartment Annick phoned. "Fred called, he wants to see me. You have any idea what it's about?"

"I think he just wants to sleep with you."

"Really? I thought it was maybe something about . . ." She stopped herself, to my immense relief. "About something else."

"No, I'm quite sure. I got the impression that's what you wanted as well."

"I suppose . . . if it doesn't bother you?"

"Why would it bother me?"

"No reason." There was a defiant lack of disappointment in her tone. "I suppose I'm going to have to break up with Bruno before long."

"Do it gently. The boy's just lost his father."

"You're right. Still, life goes on, right?"

"Right."

I hung up and put my hand between Marie-Laure's knees, and for just a moment I became self-conscious about Balthazar's being up front. Then I remembered that Balthazar knew all about it, probably knew a lot worse things about Marie-Laure than her sexual habits.

And of course he knew I'd bought a gun.

• • •

After a quick, not to say perfunctory screwing, I left Marie-Laure in her apartment. Balthazar had had the good sense to wait for me downstairs, and less than an hour after going up he was driving me back to the apartment in the sixth.

"So you have any more trouble with that fuck tried to brain you the other week?"

"Not a bit," I said, reasoning that my encounter with him in Ginny's suite didn't really qualify as "trouble."

"That's good," he said.

• • •

I was tired when I got into the apartment but not terribly so given my lack of sleep over the last twenty-four hours. I was still a little horny, even, and so it was with mixed emotions that I greeted Esmée, stark naked in the salon watching television and absently pleasuring herself with what appeared to be a vibrating egg.

"This would look very bad if anyone were to find out, you know," I told her.

"I know," she said. "Doesn't that make it that much more exciting?"

• • •

So it did. Fucking Esmée that night was one of the most thrilling sexual experiences I've ever had, coming as it did with the knowledge that we were risking serious jail time (of course it would have been even more exciting back home in the States, where we both would have been putting ourselves at risk for lethal injection). Never mind that I'd already screwed Marie-Laure earlier in the evening; I felt as though I hadn't ejaculated in a month, and Esmée writhed on the bed like a creature possessed. If you ever get the chance to fuck someone with whom you're complicit in a recent murder, I highly recommend it.

JEUDI, DIX-NEUF MAI

WE AWOKE IN THE MORNING WITH THE BED a disaster area, our clothes and underwear torn and strewn about the room, our smells all over one another. She showered and quickly dressed and left, and neither one of us spoke a word as she did so. I showered in my turn, and when I'd dressed I found Inspector Bonnot sitting in the living room.

"I hope I didn't frighten you," he said.

"Not at all," I replied, the very embodiment of aplomb.

"I ran into Mme. Guiteau as she was leaving. She graciously let me in."

"I see."

"You should have told me from the start that you were fucking her."

"I was protecting her reputation."

He chuckled. "Such as it is. Well, I knew anyway; so did all the neighbors. So, presumably, did Guiteau himself."

"He never indicated any such thing to me."

"But he wouldn't, would he?"

"I suppose not."

The inspector stood, moved to the window, and opened it up. "Do you mind if I smoke?"

"Go ahead. It's not my apartment, of course."

"No, of course." With great deliberation he stuffed and lit a pipe and began puffing lungfuls of smoke out the window and into the cool Parisian air. "I hear stories about you."

"What kind of stories?"

"All kinds. Mostly because people notice you. They tend to remember when the subject of an anecdote is a well-known personality. For example, there was a fight outside the nightclub downstairs, shortly after you moved in. Remember?"

"Vaguely."

"Vaguely? You gave the boy a concussion."

"He followed me into the building's lobby and attacked me."

"That's not the way he tells it. Still, when he checked into the hospital later no one believed his story that he'd been beaten up by none other than Dr. Crandall Taylor."

"One of the advantages of celebrity, I suppose."

"Yes, I suppose." He took a deep drag, and the smell of tobacco was quite comforting, bringing back memories of my grandfather and his brother, both smokers who went to early graves. "And of course we already know that when Bruno Guiteau tried to jump you, you gave him a very thorough beat-down in return."

"As you point out, he did jump me."

"Quite so, and he bears you no particular ill-will for it." Holding the pipe in the vicinity of the window, he thumbed through a stack of reports. "And there's this. A rather savage attack on a group of marginal young people down by the Seine. Now this, too, appears to have been a case of self-defense, but what's interesting is that these kids swore that you were the one who fought them so savagely. Naturally at the time no one took it seriously."

"Seems everyone who checked into a hospital that week was blaming me for their injuries."

He laughed. "Just so, just so. I took the liberty of looking into your background."

"You should have called my press agent, she'd have sent you the whole package."

"Yes, quite. I did go through a lot of the entertainment press. The tabloids, the TV magazines, that sort of thing. But I didn't find much of use beyond your latest triumph on the stage. Congratulations, by the way. I understand your *Tartuffe* was quite well received in Chicago."

"Thank you. I wish you could have seen it."

"Where I struck gold was when I contacted the United States Embassy and requested your military records."

I was a bit taken aback. "They handed them over as quickly as that?"

"Not so quickly. I've been working on this whole business since the day you were attacked. As I said, the divisionnaire . . ."

"Yes, his wife's a big fan."

"And what I expected to find was the usual military record for an artist. Training films, things of that nature. But you were a Green Beret, my friend."

"I find it hard to believe that you got access to my military records in any legitimate manner that quickly."

"Legitimacy is a flexible concept, monsieur, when it comes to police work and diplomacy. Let's say that monsieur le divisionnaire's concern for your well-being opened certain doors at the Quai d'Orsay, which in turn facilitated my queries via your Department of State."

"I see."

"It's an interesting record. Nothing but praise from your superiors, the highest possible references from your superior officers, and then—quite suddenly—a less than honorable discharge. No court martial, either. Seems they gave you a choice and you took the lesser of two evils."

"I had no desire to spend the remainder of my hitch in military prison."

"Quite understandable. And here you've managed to stay out of trouble since."

"A lesson learned, Inspector. My temper cost me my military career."

"And yet you've managed to parlay that loss into great success in another career, one that millions dream of."

"I have no complaints."

Having finished his bowlful, he tapped the ashes out onto the Boulevard St. Germain below. "Well, sir, I'll bother you no more today. I'll be in touch, and naturally, if anything happens out of the ordinary . . ."

"Naturally."

• • •

Disillusioned though I was at the ease with which my government gave away my supposedly inviolate secrets, there was nothing in my military record that pointed to me as Claude Guiteau's killer, and I was confident that if Inspector Bonnot had seen through me as a man capable of violence, it wasn't necessarily a predictable leap to considering me an assassin.

• • •

I went to see a movie that afternoon, an American zombie movie in which a friend of mine played the key role of the town doctor. He had a couple of nice scenes after he'd turned into one of the undead, and I had a hearty laugh when he took a large bite out of the shoulder of a young woman dressed as a police officer. When it was over I saw I'd had a couple of text messages from Fred, urging me to call him back as soon as possible.

With some trepidation I returned his call, only to find that he'd fucked Annick three times the night before. He was beside himself with joy, and I returned to the apartment rather pleased with my efforts as a matchmaker. I'd been friends with Fred for only a few weeks now, but his life as a depressive shut-in was a thing of the past.

I had dinner with Ginny at a seafood restaurant at the Place de l'Odéon. She was mad that the hotel had quashed her efforts to get the story of her ex-husband and stalker into the papers.

"Do you know what that kind of shit is worth in terms of Internet traffic?" she asked me between bites of sole meunière. "Never mind the fact that there was a cross-dresser aspect to it, which just makes it kinkier. But no, the hotel's precious reputation is at stake, so they keep it quiet. And when I pointed out to them that I stood to lose money on the proposition, you know what they had the balls to do?"

"Offer you a settlement?" I guessed.

"Damn right!"

"I hope you took it."

"Damn right I did. Shit, though, I got to get some publicity out of this stalking business."

"So you think he broke in to steal your underwear?"

"No, that's just an occasional thing when he gets high. Mostly he's into all kinds of kinky shit, all over the place: nipple torture, electric shocks, breath play, adult diapers, you name it. And when I met him he was kind of a missionary-position type of guy, you know? I mean, I understand why he's upset about us breaking up. I ruined him for regular women."

"I can certainly understand that."

"I fucking wish we could get him to do it again, just away from that tight-assed fucking hotel this time."

I thought it over. "How would you like to attend a memorial service with me tomorrow?"

She almost had a bite of sole in her mouth, and she held it there suspended before her lips in a tentative state of delighted disbelief. "Babe, am I to understand that you are asking me out on a date to somebody's funeral?"

"If you want to call it that, yes."

She put the forkful of fish down and fell back laughing. "You are a class act."

"So I guess that's a yes?"

"Fuck, yeah. There going to be food?"

"Yeah, it's kind of a wake. Just one thing," I said. "If you wanted to let David know about it, how would you do that?"

"Ooohhh." She nodded. "I can think of ways."

"Good. Because the press is going to be there, and I can pretty much guarantee there'll be cops as well."

VENDREDI, VINGT MAI

FRED SHOWED UP FOR THE MEMORIAL AT THE Hanoi Hilton stag, since Annick hadn't given Bruno the news yet; even if she had, they reasoned, it would have been poor form to rub his nose in it at his father's memorial. Marie-Laure was there with her husband, and I was there with Ginny, who wore a form-fitting minidress through which her nipples protruded like gumdrops. The mood was festive, with a giant photograph of Claude printed on a banner hanging across one wall, the cage hanging over the dance floor minus its usual scantily clad occupant, like the riderless horse in a funeral cortege. The music was the standard horrible mélange of disco, classic rock, and techno-dance, and though Esmée was seated at a table dressed in a very sexy black outfit and playing the devastated widow very convincingly, she got up every few minutes to dance and managed never to lose her look of brooding grief, not even for the most frenetic numbers, not for a second.

A great many members of the press were there by invitation. It was commonly known that shortly before his death Claude had become passionate about the film he intended to produce for his wife to star in, and so making his memorial a media event seemed a fitting tribute to a man who had previously shunned the spotlight.

I was having trouble keeping my eyes on Ginny's face while we danced, largely because of the effect of those lovely nipples. Which is funny, since I'd spent considerable time suckling them the night before and had spent half of our limo ride over playing with them. She was in her element, being watched by most of the men in the room and not a few of the ladies. Every time a flash went off she winked at me.

"I owe you big time, if this all gets onto Gawker or *E!* or *Entertainment Tonight*," she said.

"It's nothing. You get a message to David?"

"Called his brother in Oklahoma. Told him I wanted to see David, said I'd cooked up some real kinky shit he wasn't going to believe."

"Won't he think that's suspicious, your calling him up like that?"

"No," she said. "I do shit like that all the time just to torture him. He's in love with me, the poor dumb fuck."

"Are you sure he'll tell David?"

"Course he will. He tells David everything. He told David he'd fucked me, for example, which was one of the reasons David and I started having problems. Big fucking deal, right? I mean, they're brothers."

I saw Marie-Laure dancing with her husband on the other side of the dance floor. They were dancing a little less energetically than the rest of the crowd, and I wondered what he made of his wife's life. He looked pretty miserable, but upon consideration so did she.

Soon Ginny was dancing with Fred, who looked the very picture of masculine self-confidence. As I stood at the bar I saw Annick at a corner table by herself trying hard not to watch him, and a somewhat familiar-looking young man approached me and shook my hand.

"I just wanted to say I'm sorry about jumping you," he said, and even with that rather obvious clue to his identity I was drawing a blank. Whoever he was, though, he was offering an apology, so I accepted it.

"The thing is, I'm kind of going crazy at the moment, and a lot of things just came crashing down around me at the same time. Like Annick cheating on me, Esmée cutting me off."

Aha. So this was Bruno, without his dreads now, and looking rather natty. "I understand."

"Do you? Sometimes I think if anything else goes wrong I'll go crazy. Still, I know that attacking you was wrong. I'm planning on seeing a psychiatrist soon."

"Your demeanor is very different than the last time we met," I said.

"I'm heavily medicated at the moment, sir."

I told him a truncated version of my army career and my discovery of acting as a form of therapy. He listened with interest, and then I clasped his shoulder.

"You're a good-looking young fellow. Articulate. You have a decent voice. How'd you like to be in a movie?"

• • •

I had prepared two notes. Both of them read WISHING SHE WAS YOU. When I went over to present my official condolences to Esmée, I slipped her one, and brushing past Marie-Laure a few minutes later, I left the other clasped in her palm. But of course I was leaving with Ginny, and as we made our way past the members of the press both inside and out I said to several of them words to the effect that this Krysmopompas fellow was a chickenshit who lacked the balls to come after me, and that I didn't expect to hear from him again.

SAMEDI, VINGT-ET-UN MAI

WE MADE A GREAT SHOW OF MOVING Ginny into a small but elegant boutique hotel off the Boulevard St. Germain, where her suite was smaller than its predecessor but filled with objets d'art and so many flowers my eyes began itching the moment we walked through the door. I made certain the press knew we'd be there, and sure enough when we stepped out of the limo there'd been a line of photographers and television cameras to publicize the event.

"You sure he'll show?" I asked her.

"Unless he smells a trap, which I don't think he will. Not when he thinks he's going to help me make a snuff video."

We looked around for the best place for me to hide and decided it was the walk-in closet. Ginny figured she'd have him thoroughly engaged in the sack before he wanted a proper tour of the suite around the room, and the slats in the door gave me a reasonably good idea of what was happening in the room outside.

But first she wanted to christen that big bed. The thing about Ginny was, she really was horny just about all the time. And what the hell, she'd left word for David to join her at five in the evening, and it was only two-thirty now.

We had left word at the desk that if M. Steinke appeared, he was to be let up immediately. Members of the press would again be waiting outside the hotel and strategically placed in the corridors outside the room to record whatever transpired, and they all knew to be in place by four-thirty just to be on the safe side.

So we all got caught with our pants down, in my case and Ginny's literally so, when the lunatic son of a bitch burst into the room at three-fifteen and found me balls-deep in his estranged wife. Ginny screamed at the sight of him, and he came at me with a butcher knife, bellowing a cuckold's pain and an avenger's joy as I rolled off the bed and onto the floor.

I had foreseen any number of scenarios I might have to deal with today, but fighting a knife-wielding assailant while I was naked wasn't among them. He was an unskilled knife-fighter, but he was high on adrenaline and who knows what else and therefore unpredictable. I grabbed for his wrist, but he sliced my forearm and I retreated. I was a little bit ashamed, to tell you the truth, at allowing a civilian to slash me like that, and I vowed it was the last time.

He was laughing like an idiot, his eyes red and wide, and I had a bad feeling he'd scored some meth or, even worse, some angel dust. "This is a snuff film, baby, and you're the star," he said.

To my dismay I saw that Ginny was actually operating a video camera from the bed. "Damn it, give me a hand here," I yelled.

"Fight, you fucking pussies," she yelled back, and I had the sinking sensation that I'd been had. This was indeed a snuff film she was making, whether it was her ex or me that died, and I vowed that if I survived I'd see to it that she never worked outside of porn again.

I was backing away from him when he lunged suddenly, knocking me into a side table laden with a large pitcher full of flowers. His teeth bared, he lunged at me and I rolled to the side just in time to avoid being cut by a large sliver of broken crystal.

From my prone position I kicked him in the face and felt the cartilage in his nose crunch. He dropped the knife, and I plunged it into his throat. He made a truly horrible noise as the air from his lungs escaped through it, and his carotid artery spurted bright red onto the creamy white carpet as Ginny filmed. The blood began leaking rather than pumping from the wound in his neck, and his eyes lost focus.

"Turn off that fucking camera," I said.

• • •

It didn't take long for the photographers to arrive, and the police followed shortly. By that time I'd planted enough incriminating evidence on the corpse to establish definitively his identity as Krysmopompas: a page referring to *Kamikaze 1989*, torn from a book in Fred's bookstore on German New Wave cinema, and a typewritten letter ostensibly from David Steinke explaining his need to kill me, Claude Guiteau, and anyone else who might facilitate Ginny's reentry into legit show business, thereby hurting his chances of getting her back.

"It's a good job you managed to overpower him," Inspector Bonnot said. "Myself, I'd hate to be naked and face-to-face with a knife-wielding homicidal maniac."

"It's no picnic, Inspector," I agreed, and when he'd wrapped up his duties and the body had been shipped off to the Institut Médico-Légal, we repaired to the headquarters of the Police Judiciaire, where I had the rare honor of a visit from the divisionnaire himself, who was kind enough to have sandwiches and beer sent up from the café on the Place Dauphine to thank me for the autographed picture, which had delighted his wife. After I'd made my official statement, Inspector Bonnot joined me for an apéritif at that same café.

• • •

"It's funny," he said, after one of the inevitable interruptions, this time by an elderly couple who wanted, as usual, to know why I sounded so different in person than on the TV. "You're very good-natured about the whole thing. That old bitch interrupted you in midsentence."

"How can I be mean when they're so happy to meet me? It's thanks to people like her that I don't have to wait tables or drive a truck."

"True. Nonetheless, she was out of line."

"Maybe. People get flustered when they meet someone famous."

"So what are your plans now? Staying in France?"

"I certainly hope so. I just gave up a good TV role to stay here and push to get this movie made."

"Ah, that's right, your movie. The one the late M. Guiteau was going to finance."

"Exactly."

"I suppose you're out of luck there, now that he's dead."

"Maybe, maybe not. If the estate's settled quickly enough, I'm sure Esmée will step in for her husband as financial backer."

"I suppose that makes sense. Of course the whole film business is quite oblique to me."

"It's oblique to people who've spent their lives in it. Every film gets set up differently, and every television show. There's only one rule that never changes."

"And what's that?"

"Every man for himself."

• • •

We shook hands outside the café with an invitation on my part for him to visit the set once the filming was under way and walked off in opposite directions as the sun began to set. Everything had gone as planned, and it was hard to argue that the world was any the worse off without either of the men I'd killed. The movie would get made, and all involved would get what they wanted. In the distance, the lights of the Eiffel Tower sputtered on, and I felt as though Paris had been my home forever.

VENDREDI, TREIZE—

QUELQUES MOIS PLUS TARD

A FILM SET IS A SEEMINGLY CHAOTIC PLACE, if you don't know what's going on. If you do, you see that everyone is going about his business quickly and in such a way as to avoid disturbing anyone else's. First-time visitors rarely perceive this, however, and can usually be recognized by their timorous resemblance to small children crossing a busy intersection.

During our second week of production, Inspector Bonnot made, as I had invited him to, such a visit. We were on location near Paris, shooting a scene in a warehouse full of supposedly stolen artworks (Esmée had put Fred in touch with one of her late husband's contacts, a high-end art fence, who had supplied him with a wealth of useful information). I introduced Bonnot to the production assistants, to the director and cinematographer, to some of the actors he hadn't already met. He greeted Esmée solicitously and Ginny warmly (yes, I'd forgiven her for her willingness to see me killed on camera—one night with her and you'd understand why) and sat with us for lunch, after which he asked for a moment of my time, alone.

As luck would have it the scene being shot after lunch was one of the few I wasn't in. We walked along the banks of the Seine in silence for a while, and then he cleared his throat to speak.

"You know, you could have been more careful."

"How's that?" I asked.

"You left the rubber ball in his mouth, for one thing. Your prints were on the strap. So were Mme. Guiteau's. So were those of M. LaForge. And those of an unidentified fourth person, as well as those of M. Guiteau himself. His prints are explained by a second dental imprint on the ball itself—those of Mme. Guiteau."

"How did you come to get our prints?"

"There are various means of getting those, if you're not worried about it holding up in court. In your case, I swiped a drinking glass from the Guiteaus' apartment."

"I see."

"In addition, you bought a gun for five hundred euros from a certain Gégé, who likes to stay on good terms with the police. When he heard that you were involved in the Krysmopompas case he came to me."

"I did no such thing."

"You should have had your friend LaForge buy the gun. Your attempt at discretion left a good deal to be desired, my friend. Because Gégé identified the gun's previous owner, we have its ballistics, and they match those of the bullet that killed Guiteau."

We both slowed down at the sight of something in the water. I saw a thin ribcage floating in the weeds, and for a horrifying moment I thought it was a child.

"Look at that," Bonnot said. "A dead swan."

And then I saw the white feathers and the remains of the webbed feet. "So it is," I said, and we continued on our way.

"Finally, there's that name. Krysmopompas. There's the film, *Kamikaze 1989*, of course, and I found a rock group that had taken its name from the film. But you know what my first hit was when I plugged the word into Google? The *New York Times* crossword puzzle."

"Is that so?"

"Which runs every day in the *International Herald Tribune*. The word appeared as an answer therein the very day you were attacked. If, indeed, you were attacked. On several occasions I've noticed you working on the puzzle in your spare time."

The funny thing at that moment was, I'd always wondered why he hadn't picked up on those things. All of them had occurred to me as possible keys to my downfall, and I honestly never underestimated the man. I was almost relieved to find that he was as sharp as I'd thought.

"So why bring this up now, now that there's a film in production and people counting on me to make a living? Surely you knew all these things months ago."

"That's true. I suppose I wanted to come up and see a film being made. I've never been on a movie set."

"Are you going to arrest me now?"

He laughed. "If I were going to arrest you, I'd have done it before Guiteau was in the ground. He was a pig. Shall we start back?"

We turned around and walked in silence until we reached the carcass of the swan. "Seeing it like that, you realize what a large animal a swan really is," he said.

"That's true. Whereas the skeleton of a lion or a bear, stripped of flesh and fur, seems quite small by comparison to its living form."

"You're a philosopher," he said.

"So won't you be in trouble, failing to solve the murder?"

"Not every murder is solved. And speaking of trouble, I believe I mentioned that the divisionnaire's wife . . ."

"Right."

We walked along, and the already beautiful day seemed to have taken on a new glow. I was a lucky man and I knew it, but this was beyond luck.

And then he cleared his throat.

"Ah, there's just one more thing. I almost forgot."

I wondered if he did this in all his interviews, or if he'd been saving the Columbo routine for just such an occasion as mine. "What's that?"

"My daughter Jeannine, she's twenty-three years old, went to drama school, hasn't had much luck getting cast since. I was just thinking, maybe . . ."

"You know, that's funny," I said as we approached the set. "There's a role we haven't cast yet, that of a young girl." Actually it hadn't been written yet, but Fred was quick and he would understand the urgency of the matter. "Have her come by with a head shot."

"It so happens I brought one with me," Bonnot said, and from his jacket pocket he produced an eight-by-ten glossy of a young woman of considerable beauty, the kind who would be just fine onscreen even if she couldn't act her way out of a paper bag, the kind whose performance in the sack would redeem any kind of hamming on-screen.

We shook hands as though we were the best of friends, and he took off to watch the scene being shot. I climbed into my trailer for a brief nap, a massage, and a quick blowjob from Ginny before my next scene.

• • •

It's good to be the star.

Fin